MIDLIFE CURSES

WITCHING HOUR BOOK ONE

CHRISTINE ZANE THOMAS

CHRISTINE ZANE THOMAS

BOOK ONE

This is a work of fiction. Similarities to real people, places, or events are entirely coincidental.

For Jenn.

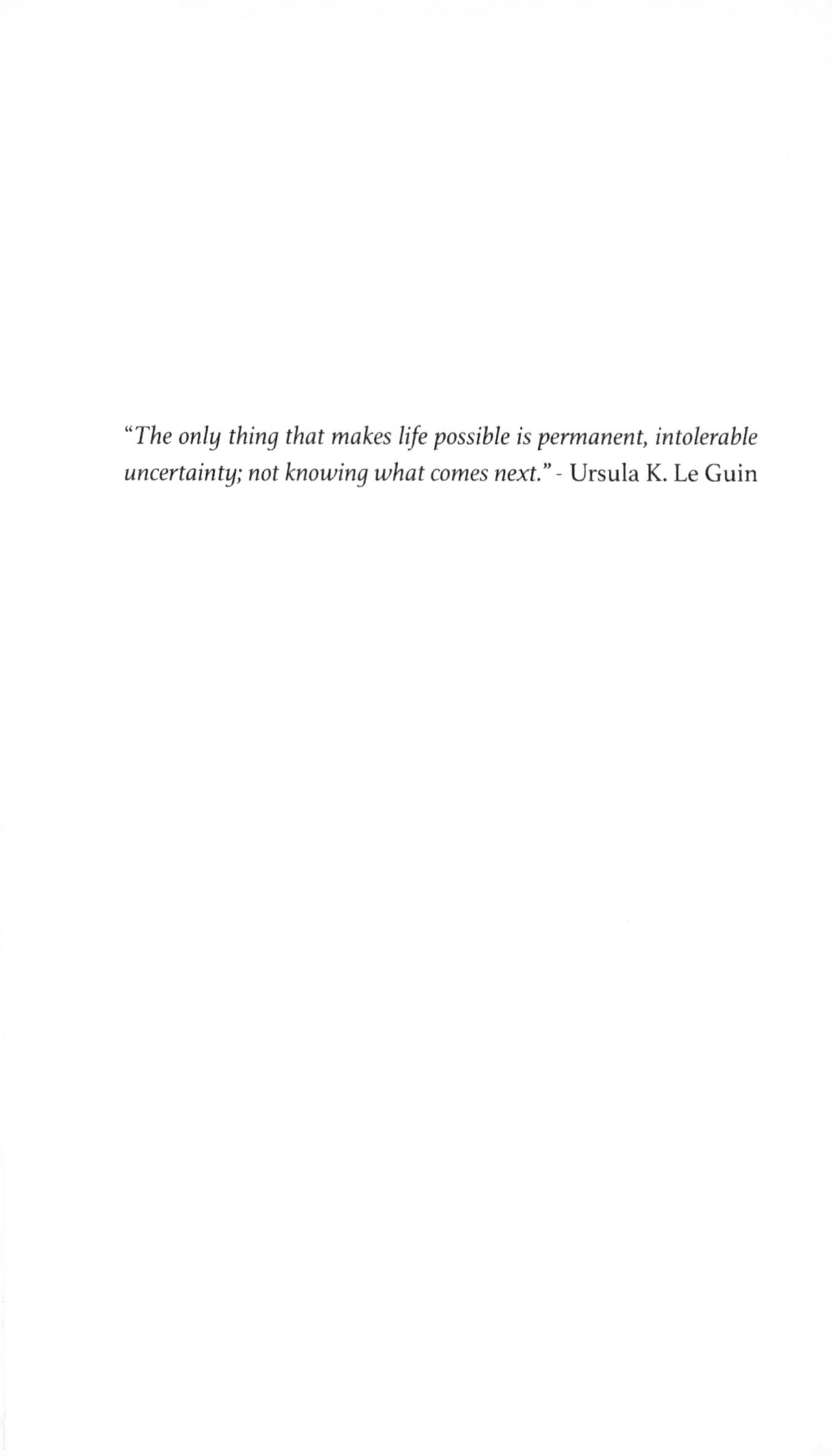

“The only thing that makes life possible is permanent, intolerable uncertainty; not knowing what comes next.” - Ursula K. Le Guin

1

IN WITCH I FILE FOR DIVORCE

I stared at the email sitting at the top of my inbox. It made my insides want to leap to the outside, only I couldn't pinpoint exactly why. At first glance, it looked completely benign. Only four words: "Meet me in five."

But I was on my hundredth glance. I stared at those words until my eyes blurred. I was still unable to glean any more information out of them.

Those four words were in reply to a standard company email—software requirements for a new client. I'd asked to be CC'd on any correspondence between our sales and engineering team. At a small company like Swizzled Innovators, that meant I was added to an email between just two people —Melissa, our sales rep, and Mark, the head of engineering. Oh, and Mark also happened to be my husband.

We'd started working there the same day. It was his idea, following several of his "brogrammer" friends from Yahoogle.

I wondered if Mark had made a mistake—if he'd hit *reply all* accidentally. An easy mistake to make—one I'd made in the past, often to my detriment.

I watched the door to his office, the one adjacent to my own. Back when we'd started at the company, we shared a small office. Back then, it was fun. Working all hours at a startup hadn't seemed like a chore.

Where is this meeting going to take place? I wondered. *Is it a meeting at all or something else?*

Maybe Mark and Melissa get coffee together all the time. It weirded me out how easily *Mark and Melissa* rolled off the tongue—even in my head. In fact, it was so weird it made me shudder.

There's no "Mark and Melissa," I told my inner monologue. Or perhaps it told me.

Right on time, Mark left his office. I pretended not to notice. *Oh, here's my computer that just went to sleep.* From the corner of my eye, I saw him glance my way, but he didn't seem worried at all. That was a good sign.

I had to stand to see where he went next—to the meditation room. The dark one-person only meditation room.

Not a minute passed before Melissa scurried that way, stumbling on her too-high heels. She was awkward and self-conscious as a rule, but I could swear she used that trip as a ruse, to gauge if anyone was watching her.

I ducked behind my door before the tall brunette could see me. Melissa flipped the sign on the meditation room from vacant to occupied and slipped into the dark room.

The room had once been used for lactating mothers, when there was a lactating mother. Now, it was supposed to be for moments of quiet reflection. There was a fish tank, a white noise machine, and two cozy beanbags. It was a perfect storm. A storm I wasn't quite ready to face.

A few minutes later, I watched them leave. *Only* minutes. I knew Mark. He wasn't one to worry about anyone else's needs. In a way, it was funny. Melissa probably thought *quickie* meant something regarding time.

I resigned myself to confronting him that night. My heart wasn't breaking. It was crumbling into pieces as I went back to my desk.

And I would've waited—I really would have—had I not caught them sneaking in there again later that afternoon.

This time, I couldn't sit idly by. I couldn't ignore it happening multiple times right under my nose.

Adrenaline coursing through my veins, I basically flew out of my office. And before I gave myself a chance to think about it, I knocked on the meditation room door.

In the tone I reserve for company meetings—my most demanding voice—I said, "Mark, I need to see you *right now*. It's urgent."

Heart pounding in my chest, I stormed down the hall toward the breakroom, unsure where to go, unsure what to do.

This wasn't the plan.

The plan was to open a bottle of wine and to calmly but assertively ask Mark for a divorce. Still seeing red, I was anything but calm.

"Constance," Mark said. "Constance, it's not what you think."

Mark trailed me like a dog with its tail between its legs. Except Mark's tail was a belt dangling from his halfway down pants. He jerked them to his waist, zipped the zipper, clasped the belt, and said, "Okay, it *is* what you think. But I can explain."

My stomach churned and was on the edge of evicting its contents onto the grimy breakroom floor. My eyes stung. Still, I resolved to keep it together, to put on a brave face—

mostly because nearly half of the company was watching from their desks.

This stupid open office floor plan. The tears began to flow down my cheeks.

I should've seen this coming. A little voice in the back of my mind said *it* had. It said *I told you—I told you he was up to something.*

Only, that little voice wasn't so loud a week ago. It hadn't warned the rest of me—the parts of my body doing all the work, pulling air into my lungs and pumping blood from my chest. Had those parts known, well, maybe I wouldn't have ended up a red-faced monster with mascara smeared down my cheeks and snot cascading from my nose.

My thick blonde hair was frizzed where I twisted it in frustration—an attempt to subvert my hands, to keep them from throttling Mark's highly throttle-able neck.

"It's not you, it's me," Mark said twice. The first in an undertone, the second, loud enough for Steve in accounting to hear. Accounting was in the back by the stairs.

Strike one and strike two. Obviously, it's him. Who else could it be?

Given the way he—and everyone else—was looking at me, that answer, too, was obvious.

But I couldn't let him win. He was just reeling off the same played out, cliché-of-a-phrase he'd heard in every romantic movie ever made. Not that Mark had many of those. Six, maybe seven. And they were all comedies starring Adam Sandler.

"Of course it's you," I retorted. "I'm not the one who had my pants down with Melissa."

"It's not Melissa's fault either," Mark said chivalrously.

"Again, I know," I reiterated. "It's your fault and *yours* alone."

"Well," Mark muttered, "not alone. I mean, you're to blame for this too, right? It takes two to tango and all that. And it's obvious there are some *things* that I haven't been getting from our marriage."

I knew exactly what *things* he was talking about.

"There's more to a relationship than sex," I said.

"Keep your voice down, Constance." First, he had the audacity to blame me, then he tried to shush me.

Mark tried to put a hand on my shoulder. Reflexively, I pulled away. I knew that lowering our voices wasn't going to help anything. The whole office could see and hear us. Some even had the temerity to walk by, their ears pricked like Doberman Pinschers.

Granted, it was the middle of the day, and one or two probably wanted to retrieve their lunches from the office refrigerator. But most were there for the spectacle, lurking to get the inside scoop on the drama.

I took a deep breath, then took in the scene. My formerly blue eyes—now undoubtedly red and blue—scanned the open floor plan. Every single person pretended to be busy all of a sudden, unwilling to look at me. Except Melissa, who was already back at her workstation with earbuds in her ears. She wasn't listening to our argument. She pretended the confrontation had nothing to do with her. And maybe it didn't.

Maybe this is all my fault.

Then Mark spoke, and I knew better. This was *his* fault. I should've seen it coming. I could've shielded myself from this inevitability.

"It not *just* the lack of sex," he whispered. "It takes a lot of work to, uh, make a relationship work. It's been ten years. It's not working."

"I know, Mark," I said, mimicking his tone. "I was there

too. We were working—working on this company. That's all we've been doing the past few years."

"Yeah, well, that's what I'm trying to say," he pleaded. "We're here at work together, but you'd never know that we're married. You're always busy. Then we get home, and you go straight to sleep like you're exhausted."

"I *am* busy. And I go to sleep because I *am* exhausted."

"Right, but can't you see why I wanted to—I needed to—to sleep with someone else?"

"Oh, you weren't doing much sleeping." Brody Hickman couldn't hold his tongue any longer. He barged into the breakroom and refilled his coffee cup, officially making the breakroom, and our personal lives, fair game.

A gaggle of employees streamed inside. They opened the refrigerator, shouldered into a line at the microwave, and like Brody, poured coffee into their cups, all of which had our company logo on the side.

This was why I should never have taken a job with all of Mark's friends and none of my own. I should've done something else with my life, not tried to micromanage code jockeys.

It was too much. I wanted them gone. I wanted everyone to just stop. So, I yelled, "Stop it—all of you!"

And they did. Everyone just stopped—even Mark.

It was more than just a pause though. Much more. They froze, unmoving.

It was a relief at first. The weirdness of it took a few seconds for my brain to comprehend.

I tentatively waved my hand in front of Mark's face. He didn't blink.

It was like on *Saved by the Bell* when Zach Morris said "time out" and everyone around him stopped what they were doing.

Only that was a TV show and this was real life.

My life.

I was starting to freak out. This couldn't be real. Then it clicked into place. I realized my words caused this.

I screamed.

I screamed again, loud and long, wishing for things to go back to normal.

And everything did.

Well, sort of. Mark and the staff unpaused, but now they were looking at me, wondering why I was screaming like I'd just met Pennywise the Dancing Clown.

Brody took a sip of his coffee. "Why the hell is the coffee cold?"

FIFTEEN MINUTES LATER, Randy, the HR manager, was in *my* office telling *me* that it wasn't working out. Randy's words were the human resources equivalent to Mark's "it's not you, it's me."

Two hours after that, I was in another office—the office of my attorney. And Mark was served divorce papers the next day.

I wasn't going to wait around for the full six-month waiting period required by California law for the divorce to be final. I let Mark have everything—the house with its three hundred and twenty-five more payments, and the Tesla that I'd helped secure. And everything else he wanted —the TV, the other TV, the video game consoles, and our shared collection of Funko POPs. Well, except for the *Harry Potter* POPs, those were mine.

I packed up Crookshanks, my fifteen-year-old Subaru

Outback—the only car that was solely mine, the one I'd had since college—and I left.

I started toward my Dad's place in San Diego. But somewhere along the way, I changed my mind.

I let Mark have the whole state. I just kept driving without anywhere in particular in mind. I stopped to sleep. I stopped to eat. But I didn't consult a map or a phone. I was driving on autopilot.

Two days later, I was surprised to find myself on an unfamiliar doorstep. My memory of the road trip faded into nothing. I couldn't remember what roads I'd taken or what hotels I'd stayed in. Nothing. I had no recollection of how exactly I'd gotten here or where *here* was. I had no clue who was on the other side of that door.

But I knocked on it anyway.

I thought about running back to the car, but my feet might as well have been nailed to the porch. I couldn't go back.

The door cracked open and a narrow slice of an old woman's face appeared. She was smiling.

"Constance," my estranged grandmother—Gran—said, pulling the door wide. "I've been expecting you."

2

IN WITCH I GET CAUGHT SPEEDING

G*reat—just great,* I thought. *As if this day, this week, this whole year, could get any worse than it already is.*

Blue strobe lights illuminated the whole street. The lights bounced off walls and windows and trees. The asphalt glowed blue.

I pulled Crookshanks onto the shoulder, slammed her into park, and rolled down my window. The engine whined —her way of saying "it wasn't me that did anything wrong. It was you! Your foot on the pedal."

The car had a point. I turned off the ignition.

It was still dark outside, ten minutes to six. I had to be at work at 6:00 a.m.

The job was new, something Gran had set up for me along with her spare bedroom—no questions asked, just saying she'd been expecting me.

When I asked her why, she changed the subject and left my question unanswered. Every time I tried to circle back, she deflected me easily, with things like where I could find an easy job. After working myself to the bone in Silicon Valley, an easy job sounded pretty good.

She'd failed to mention this easy job started at the crack of dawn.

A tinge of gray light peeked over the sloping horizon. What passed as a mountain in Virginia amazed me. Still, there was beauty in them, and the hills kept the temperature moderately cool for it being so close to summer.

The silhouette of a sheriff's deputy strode through the blue light toward my window. I half-expected him to shine a flashlight in my face, but he stopped just behind the door and leaned toward the window, bent at the waist. His hand rested on the holster at his hip.

In the dim light, I could just make out his features. He had dark hair, cut short under a ball cap. His mustache was thick and disorderly, framing his mouth—it was definitely out of regulations. There was a growth of stubble on his chin and cheeks that made me wonder why he bothered shaving at all. Despite his grizzly appearance, he was attractive. Lean. Dark eyes, a thin nose. Scrunching his mustached lips together tightly, he studied me.

He probably wondered why he didn't recognize me here in Creel Creek, Virginia—the smallest town I'd ever set foot in. Or worse, he thought I was passing through and thus an easy target for his speed trap.

I wondered if I was supposed to start the conversation. After all, we both knew what he was going to say. Finally, he asked, "So how fast do you think you were going back there?"

If I knew that, I thought, *I probably wouldn't be in this predicament.*

"I don't know. You tell me, deputy."

He smiled. His teeth gleamed in the gray light. "Ma'am,

you may not be aware, but this is a thirty-five mile-per-hour zone. And I'm not a deputy. I'm the sheriff."

I was taken aback. *Since when does a sheriff write speeding tickets? Since when is a sheriff so young?* There was no way this man was a day over forty. Who did he think he was, Andy Griffith?

This wasn't the first time in my short stay that Creel Creek had reminded me of the little town of Mayberry. But where Mayberry was quaint and charming, Creel Creek was charmless and dull.

"Well, *Sheriff*," I said, a tad snippy, "if you don't mind my asking, how fast was I going?"

"About fifty," he replied with a shake of his head. "And if you don't mind me asking, can you produce your license, insurance, and registration?"

"Of course." I gathered them up and passed them through the window. This was where I knew things would get worse. He'd seen my California tag, and now my California license. It was a total lie to say I hadn't had the time to run by the DMV and change them. Since moving to my Gran's house, I'd had nothing but time. Until last week, when I'd finally gotten off my butt and took her up on that job. Not a very good job, mind you. Easy, though.

The sheriff shot me another smile, but this time his mustache did most of the work. Then he strode back to his SUV.

It was eerily quiet. The strobing lights danced, reflecting off every possible surface, the cars, the leaves, and the road signs in the distance.

If I was counting, and I *was* counting, this was my third week in this Virginia hamlet. East of Kentucky and just below the border of West Virginia, Creel Creek was almost ghost town quiet.

When I left California, I'd left with the intention of starting my life over—of hitting the reset button. But the past few weeks hadn't been easy. They were the icing on the misery cake, the stale yellow cake that had been one of the worst years of my life.

My mind raced back to that day—the day everything came apart. Then the door of the deputy's SUV creaked. This time he came to a stop at my window. I could make out just a hint of his Old Spice deodorant. This man wasn't the type to wear cologne. He was simple, a lot like the town itself.

"I'm going to let you off with a warning... this time." He handed the documents back but held on to my license.

"Thanks, I guess," I said. The clock on the dashboard told me I was already four minutes late for work.

"You guess, huh?" He laughed. "I can scoot on back there and write you out that ticket if you want me to."

"There's no need for that," I said.

He smiled, then shook his head. "Do I know you from somewhere? We didn't grow up together, did we?"

"I don't think so," I told him. "Unless you grew up in California."

"No," he said. "But I know you from somewhere."

Unlikely, I thought. I could count on one hand the number of people I knew in Creel Creek. And as much as I appreciated not getting a ticket, sitting here while he pictured every blue-eyed blonde girl he'd ever met wasn't getting either of us anywhere.

"Sorry," I said. "It's just, I'm late for work—"

"That's it!" he said triumphantly. "That's where I know you from."

"From work?" I asked skeptically. I had not been, nor ever planned to be, a sheriff.

"Not *my* work," he said. "*Your* work. You work down at the grocery, right?"

"I do. I did." *Hint, hint.*

Normally, I'd wonder if something was off with me, not recognizing a customer, especially such a memorable one—the mustache, the dark eyes, the nice smile. But I'd found it was best not to let my eyes linger on any of our shoppers for too long. There wasn't a Walmart in Creel Creek, but the grocery's clientele more than made up for it. I was thinking of starting my own website, *People of Creel Creek.*

"That explains it," he said, nodding. "See, I know everyone around here. And I didn't know you, Constance Campbell." He read the name from my license before slipping it into my waiting palm. "For a second this morning, I thought you might be passing through. But your face—it was so familiar."

"Well, I'm glad we got that figured out," I said. "It's just I, uh—"

"You have to get to work," he said with a nod.

I had everything back. And he did say he was giving me a warning. I wondered if I zoomed off right now if I would get into any trouble.

"I'm Sheriff Marsters, by the way. Sheriff David Marsters. You can call me Dave, if you like."

"Sheriff Dave," I repeated.

"Just Dave." His mustache bristled with a different smile. There was something shy about it. It would've been kind of cute if he wasn't ruining my day before it even started.

"It was nice meeting you, *just* Dave," I said.

Now, would you let me leave...

"You, too, Constance." He tipped his ball cap toward me. "You have a great day, now. I'll be seeing you around."

I wasn't sure if that was a friendly remark or a police

warning. While part of me hoped I *would* see him again, another was uneasy at the thought. There was something about police officers that always made me uncomfortable—like I was going to slip up and break a few laws in their presence, get arrested, and spend the rest of my days in prison. Seeing one on the highway made me practically forget how to drive. Seeing one in a bank made me feel like I'd just robbed it but forgotten about the getaway.

After he got in his SUV, I eased Crookshanks out onto the road. Not a single car had passed us, and there wasn't another for the remainder of the drive to the grocery. Like everything else about Creel Creek this time of the morning, it was dead.

3

IN WITCH I'M LATE FOR WORK

I sprinted across the parking lot, now a full fifteen minutes late for my shift. Like the road, the lot was empty except for the few cars parked in the very back. Mr. Caulfield, the grocery's owner-slash-manager, insisted that the employees park as far away from the store as possible to leave spots available for our customers. While an okay policy in general, those extra seconds I spent crossing from one side to the other made me that much later.

I heaved a relieved sigh when I saw that the lot was also devoid of his ugly green Mustang. Said policy didn't account for why Mr. Caulfield's reserved spot—the one with his picture on it—was the spot adjacent to the two painted for the handicapped.

Slowing my pace to a jog, I stutter-stepped, waiting for the sluggish automatic doors to jerk open. This morning, the world was against me.

I should have turned around and gone back to bed before anything else swooped my way.

The store's air conditioning sent a shiver down my now sweaty spine. As in most grocery stores, I was greeted by a row of registers just inside the entrance. It being a small store there were five, only two of which were manned at any given time.

The produce section was around to the right. Behind the registers were the aisles that every diet book tells you to avoid. The far wall was home to the butcher's counter. It took up a whole side of the store and carried everything—in quantity. As far as I know, it's the only place to buy meat in a fifty-mile radius.

Jade the butcher—no, not her serial killer name—was behind the display case portioning out prefilled deli meat bags.

Working at the grocery, like living with Gran, was another in the long line of questionable decisions I'd made recently. With a master's degree in business from UCLA, I'd been a project manager at three different tech firms, all of which were major players in the software industry, before moving to Swizzled Innovators with Mark.

So, why was I putting myself through this?

Well, for one, there weren't any tech companies in Creel Creek, Virginia. And while I could've found a remote position, something to do from home—from Gran's home—that just wasn't me.

I wanted—no, I needed to be around people. Or, so I thought. And for my own sanity, I had to be out of Gran's house for long stretches of time.

I didn't need the money. Not really. Not yet. But I *wanted* a mindless job to get my mind off of things—things being Mark and the divorce. The grocery fit that bill nicely. *Too nicely.*

The job was so mindless I was hearing voices in my head. On several occasions over the last week, I'd asked a customer to repeat themselves only to learn they hadn't said anything in the first place. Then I was left wondering *who* had.

Maybe it was my stank-faced coworker playing a trick on me. From her cash register, Trish tapped her finger on an imaginary watch.

Yes, I know I'm late. I wanted to shout.

She's the closest thing you have to a friend, I reminded myself. I fluttered my fingers in a halfhearted wave. My attempt to be friendly.

Besides Gran, Trish was the person in Creel Creek I knew the best. Not that that was saying much. But I'd gotten to know her a little, chatting at the registers.

Trish had a way about her. A confidence—an air like it was her way or the highway. In that regard, she reminded me of Gran.

Unlike Gran, Trish stood about a head shorter than me. I was used to that, at two inches shy of six feet, I was taller than most men.

She was around my age, maybe a little older. It was hard to tell. Her makeup reminded me of a teenage goth girl—her green eyes popped, framed in heavy black eyeliner. And not hazel green, these were a vivid emerald. Her lipstick matched the streak of violet in her otherwise black-as-night hair. It was dyed, but her roots were also dark. Maybe she was a brunette.

Based on the gray hairs I found each time I parted mine, it was time I did the same thing. Thirty-nine might not be technically over the hill, but it felt like the grinding of a roller coaster before it lets go of the track.

Ninety percent of the time, Trish communicated with gestures. She jerked her chin toward the dairy refrigerators in the back of the store and raised her eyebrows at me.

I managed to keep from rolling my eyes before she

caught me. I knew I had to clock in and count my drawer. She was acting like she wanted me to *magic* myself there and back again.

"I know," I said. "I'll clock in and be back in a jiff."

"JIF's on aisle two," Trish quipped. "And do hurry."

Honestly, she acts as if we'll be swamped with customers any minute. The only other people in the store were coworkers in their black vests, buttoned at the middle.

Hal, one of the stockers, beamed when he saw me. He was unloading cans of soup and arranging them so their labels were proudly on display.

"Uh, Constance," he said in his oddly soft voice, "you got a minute?"

"No, I've got to clock in," I told him.

"That's fine." He nodded to himself. "It can wait. I just, um, wanted to—"

I left him there to ponder those next words. I knew what he wanted to say, or had a good idea, anyway. He tried to get those same words out every day, ever since I started.

I pulled my black vest out of a breakroom cubby and pinned on my purple nametag. **Constance**, it proclaimed in bold block letters. Under it, in tiny print, was the word *cashier*.

Oh, how the mighty have fallen. I wondered what Mark would think if he saw me here, doing this.

I counted my till, then hustled back across the store. This was supposed to be a two-person job—like the second person was going to thwart a thief with a gun. Or a knife.

In those dire circumstances, I'd gladly hand over the money, all two hundred dollars of it. Mostly George Washingtons.

I detoured, circling around to the produce section. They were still no customers in sight.

Nick, the produce manager, was unloading a box of green bananas next to the speckled brown ones. I grabbed one, well past its prime, and called it breakfast.

I veered toward the register, well away from the soup aisle, but Hal caught up with me anyway.

"You all clocked in?" he asked nervously.

The answer was so obvious I didn't even acknowledge it. I made a face that I hoped would pass for a friendly smile, a smile that also said *I don't have time for this right now. Or ever.*

"It's just, uh, Constance, I was wondering—"

"Hal," I said, probably not as sweetly as I meant to, "we've been over this, haven't we? Do we really need to…?"

His face told me we were going to have this conversation not only today but probably tomorrow and the next day and the next as well.

"Hal, I just got out of a relationship. Not just any relationship—a marriage. I'm still married. Technically. And I'm so not ready to date anyone. You're really sweet, though."

Sweet was one way to describe him. Goofy, blithering, and a little pushy were other words. He was also on the dumpy side, a tad overweight with unkempt hair. He had a bald spot and his glasses came straight from the 1980s and didn't hide the acne scars high on his cheeks. He wasn't anyone's idea of the perfect rebound.

"We wouldn't have to call it a date," he bumbled. "I mean, we could call it two friends having dinner at Orange Blossoms. I'd even let you pay for your own dinner. Their steaks are—"

"Adequate," I interjected. Like most things Creel Creek had to offer, the town's one chain restaurant was just decent but bordering on subpar.

"—fantastic." His last word came out like the final whimper of air from a balloon.

"I'm sorry, Hal. It's still a no."

"For now," he said.

"Right. For now." *And forever and ever and ever.* I felt bad for him but not bad enough to go on a date.

"Could I have your number then?" he asked. "For later, that is."

"I don't think—"

"Then you take my number. Here, I'll put in your phone. You can call me anytime, day or night."

"Fine." It seemed like the only way to get him away from me. I pulled my phone from my vest pocket—a violation of store policy—unlocked it and handed it to him.

He mumbled while he typed the digits.

"What was that?"

"There," he said with a flourish. "Call me whenever you're ready."

"Thanks." I took my phone. He'd be seeing my number light up his phone's screen at a quarter past never.

Finally, I reached my post at the express lane—fifteen items or less. To some people, that number was only a suggestion. Either that or they needed to wear flip-flops to count that high. I dropped my till in the drawer and slammed it shut. Trish huffed exasperatedly. My tardiness seemed to have put her out something fierce.

I thought she was going to come down on me. Maybe I'd get a written reprimand. Her name tag read Lead Cashier, after all. Kind of like the express lane item limit, I wasn't sure the title actually meant anything.

"What happened to you this morning?" she asked.

"I got stopped."

"Stopped?" Trish's Southern drawl was more pronounced than usual.

"For speeding."

"You're kidding," she said. "I mean, you *are* kidding, right?"

"Why would I joke about something like that?"

"Who stopped you? Man or woman?"

"Man. Sheriff."

This wasn't the first time I'd heard Trish laugh, but it was the hardest. "Dave probably hadn't even had his coffee yet. And he stopped you?" Trish shook her head. "You must've been going mighty fast."

"He did," I said. "And I wasn't. Not that fast." I sighed. It was my turn to be exasperated.

"Dave didn't give you a ticket, now, did he?"

"No, he didn't," I replied. "I guess he thought I was from out of town when he stopped me. Then he thought he knew me from somewhere—turns out, it was here. If I hadn't told him I was late for work, he probably would've given me one."

Or we'd still be talking.

"Sugar," Trish started, leaning across her conveyor belt toward me, "Dave Marsters ain't never gave no woman a ticket in his life."

Was that a double or triple negative? I wondered.

"Never? Really?"

"Never."

"What, is it like a chauvinist thing?" I asked. "Or will *he* be trying to date me next?" Even though Dave was decent, maybe bordering on cute if he shaved his mustache, all I needed was yet another local yokel pining for me. Hal was plenty.

"Doubtful." Trish straightened. "Dave hasn't dated since his wife died two years ago. He's got three little girls at home. Talk about being outnumbered. No, ever since she passed he lets them girls get away with murder. And he lets women off with a warning every time we speed through town."

"How often do you speed through town?"

"Often enough." Trish winked. "Now, Willow, his deputy, *will* give you a ticket. So be careful."

"Good to know."

This was probably the first conversation I'd had with Trish that wasn't about the store or why I'd moved to Creel Creek. We didn't exactly hit it off my first few days. And Trish, a lifelong resident of Creel Creek, had *nothing* in common with me.

I searched for something constructive to do while we waited for shoppers, opting to spray down my belt with cleaner, then review the weekly sales flyer.

Customers trickled in over the next hour.

Along with them came Mr. Caulfield. He was tall and thin, very pale, and at least a decade older than me, but his skin was smooth like he used the world's best moisturizer. His name tag read Eric, but no one dared call him that—something I'd learned on my first day—the last day I assumed we were equal. After all, I'd been a career woman until this point, one with an MBA.

Mr. Caulfield quickly put me in my place.

Today, he strolled to his office in back and didn't surface for another hour.

Outside, a fog had rolled in, blanketing the parking lot with thick smoke-like mist. Since I was on a roll with Trish, and since we weren't busy, I chanced my luck at a second conversation. This one about the life or death subject that is the weather.

"What's up with that?" I pointed outside.

"What's up with what?"

"The fog." I gestured more forcefully toward the sliding

glass doors. They opened on my command, or so I thought for a moment. Then a freckle-faced kid hopped inside, playing a game with the sensor, his mother in tow.

"Oh, that."

For a second, I thought she was going to elaborate, but she didn't, her attention caught by Hal.

He was standing in the aisle behind my register.

"It's eerie, isn't it?" He smiled broadly. His teeth were yellowish and gray. I tried not to stare. Our coworkers, Trish included, called him Halitosis Hal behind his back.

I added lack of proper hygiene to his list of cons. But other than bad breath and constantly asking me out on dates, he seemed nice enough.

"It is eerie," I agreed. "But why is it like this *every* day? Is it just in the spring?"

"It's not *every* day," Hal objected. "Just most days. It's called valley fog. There's a scientific reason for it and everything. I have a book on it, if you'd like to—"

"She'll pass," Trish interrupted.

"I think *she* can decide for herself." There was some animosity there I hadn't seen in him before.

"That's okay, Hal," I told him. "*She* isn't big on reading nonfiction." I turned to Trish and said, again in the third person, "And she can handle things herself."

"Noted," Trish said. Maybe she had been doing me a favor, coming to my aid.

If I didn't know better, I might think Trish was starting to like me.

Our impromptu gathering was broken up when Mr. Caulfield appeared behind Hal.

"Am I paying you three to talk?" he asked.

He did this sometimes, appearing from nowhere. His footsteps were all but silent, and he was somehow able to evade the large bowl mirrors on aisles one and ten, the store's blind spots.

"No, sir, you aren't," Hal answered.

"Thank you, Hal. We'll call this your smoke break, then. Now, please get back to stocking."

"Sir," I protested. I didn't know if Hal smoked, but given his teeth I thought there was a high likelihood. "Don't take his break away. He was just telling me about the fog. It's my fault—I asked about it."

"He was?" Mr. Caulfield tilted his head contemplatively. "And what did Hal say about the fog?"

"He said there's a book on it." I shrugged. "He said it's something called—what did you say—valley fog?"

"It's a *naturally* occurring phenomenon," Trish added helpfully.

Mr. Caulfield pursed his lips. "That it is," he said. "That'll be all, Hal. And you two—" He leveled his gaze at Trish and me. "Isn't there something you can do to occupy your time other than yapping?"

"There sure is." Trish smiled.

I nodded, wondering exactly what she meant. I'd already read the weekly sales. There wasn't much left to do aside from ring up customers.

It was like Mr. Caulfield read my mind.

"Constance," he said, "I want you to study the produce chart. I like my cashiers to know the codes, not have to look it up every time a customer brings them a butternut squash."

"Four-seven-five-nine," Trish blurted.

Mr. Caulfield stared into my eyes—so hard, I wanted to look away. But I couldn't. It was like I was trapped. "And you're not going to make this a regular thing, are you?"

Perplexed, I made a questioning face, still unable to look away.

Again, it was like he read my thoughts.

"You were late this morning. I know salaried jobs allow a certain amount of flexibility. You're probably used to coming in anytime you want. But it's not like that here. You clock in on time, and you leave on time."

Just like you do, I thought derisively. His eyes narrowed, but he didn't say anything.

"No, it's not going to be a habit," I said meekly.

"That's what I like to hear." He glided away.

Either he'd checked my timecard or, more likely, he'd watched the surveillance camera footage of me dashing through the parking lot fifteen minutes late. He was probably headed back to his office to do more of the same. Watching the store cameras was like his hobby.

Frustrated, I opened the binder beside the register.

Bananas, four-zero-one-one.

MY SHIFT ENDED in the early afternoon. I was returning my vest to its cubby when raised voices from Mr. Caulfield's office pricked my ears.

I tried not to be nosy. I tried to look the other way. But it wasn't my fault I could hear almost every word.

"I told you," a woman's voice said, "I couldn't work tonight. I have something else planned. It's why I came in early. We talked about this."

"We did." Mr. Caulfield's voice wasn't loud, but his baritone cut through the closed door anyway. "And I told you, I'd think about changing the schedule."

"You know that typically means yes."

"But this time it meant no. I need you back here tonight. Only for a few hours."

"Well, I can't," she said. "I have something personal to do."

"And that is?"

"It's personal. Hence, I'm not telling you."

Jade, the butcher, stormed out of his office.

"I'm not asking," Mr. Caulfield called after her. "You'll be here tonight." But she was already out of earshot.

4

YER A WITCH, CONSTANCE

My grandmother lived on the outskirts of Creel Creek in a subdivision just past a cemetery. Her house was small and cramped and a perfect candidate for the show *Hoarders*. Unmaintained for several decades, clutter and spent cardboard boxes were piled up everywhere.

So, when I wasn't at work, I did projects around her house—recycling the boxes, fixing a leaky faucet or two, unclogging the disposal, and dozens of minor but necessary tasks to undo the neglect.

I even weeded her garden, which had been populated solely by weeds. If I was going to live here, I wanted to grow my own herbs, cook my own food, and pay my own way.

Gran liked my initiative and my spunk. Unfortunately, those were about the only things she liked. She had criticism for everything else—my hair, my complexion, and even my cooking. This from a woman who could barely heat up a Stouffer's Mac and Cheese.

If the new job and the new town weren't enough, my grandmother might just chase me back to California.

Like me, Gran was tall. We were both in the middle between thin and curvy. Gran's gray hair curled to just past her ears. When she was younger, it had been strawberry blonde, and there were still some reddish highlights.

I'd only visited Gran once in my life—the summer before I turned thirteen. Three years after my mother's passing.

Gran, my mother's mother, never ventured to California. Not even for the funeral.

I only have vague memories of my mother. Most of what I know is secondhand, things my father told me. He was still kicking around in San Diego, enjoying the retired life. We FaceTimed a lot.

I probably would've left Gran and gone home to Dad had I not seen this place with my own eyes. It wasn't just the *house* that needed tending, Gran needed someone too. And that someone might as well be me, her only living relative.

We'd reconnected when she got "the Facebook." Her words, not mine. It was probably around that same time she'd learned how to order things online. There was a new stack of boxes waiting on the patio when I got home from work.

I took them inside and left them in the hall. Eight hours on my feet had me ready to put them up.

Gran was in her La-Z-Boy. Despite the temperature outside hovering around eighty and the inside air only a smidgen below that, she had a quilt wrapped around her feet.

Her chair was about five feet from her television, one of the old tube kind. Her eyes were glued to it.

I fell onto, not into, the hard couch on the other side of the den.

The *Harry Potter* movie music trumpeted from stereo

speakers attached to the TV. Gran had been rummaging through my DVD collection again.

"I don't care what these movies say," she complained. "You don't become a witch until you turn forty. And there're no schools for it. No magic banks either, I don't think. There's just, well, there's..." She struggled a moment. "There's just magic," she ended with a whimper, not a bang.

Unprepared for one of her tirades, I tried to figure out what she was getting at. Of course there were no wizarding schools. No Gringotts, either. I'd spent the better part of my college years hoping to get my letter from Hogwarts.

My brain leaped, rejecting her claim about magic for the other thing she'd said. *Something about turning forty.* An odd coincidence. My own fortieth circle around the sun was a few days away from its completion—a fact I was trying to forget.

Oddly enough, I did share a birthday with someone from Hogwarts—the same *exact* date, June 5, 1980. It was my secret shame. Yes, Draco Malfoy and I were turning forty. But I'm a Ravenpuff—that's a Ravenclaw with Hufflepuff tendencies—I'm certainly no Slytherin.

Gran glared at me, trying to goad me into saying something.

I tried, "You know, Gran, these are books too, not just movies. Good books. I have them upstairs if you'd like to read them."

"That's it!" Gran slapped her knee as if I'd won the Showcase Showdown on *The Price Is Right*—her favorite show.

"Books," she said. "That's where you learn to be a witch. Spell books and potion books. Books of curses. Well, that and me—you'll have me, of course, to guide you."

"To guide me?" I asked. "What are you talking about?"

This was exactly why I'd stayed in Creel Creek. I'd begun to notice Gran often became confused. I thought it might be the onset of dementia, but I couldn't strongarm her into visiting a doctor. Not yet. That was on my list of things to do, along with the housework.

"Did you have tea this afternoon?" I asked her. "You're not yourself until you've had your tea and a little snack."

Gran wasn't like anyone else, tea or no tea. She was tough to pin down, always jabbering away about something. The problem being *something* changed with the wind—or more often.

She liked to slurp Earl Grey in the afternoon while I preferred black tea, no matter the time of day. Or wine. I'd have killed for a decent glass of wine. Only Gran didn't drink, and I'd never been one to leave a bottle half full. A bottle a day habit was just what I needed to turn this minor bout of depression into something more severe.

I wanted to get Gran off this tangent. Make us some tea, then maybe a midafternoon nap would do her—would do both of us—some good.

I turned off the television. No more *Harry Potter* for her.

Gran scowled. "I'm talking about you being a witch."

"A witch?"

"You're a witch, Constance." She said it as matter-of-factly as she'd told me about this season's cast of *Big Brother*. In fact, she'd been more excited about *Big Brother*.

"Okay, Gran." *Maybe it's low blood sugar.* I really needed to get her to see a doctor.

I hurried to put the kettle on, and to my utter surprise, she followed me and sat down at the kitchen table, permanently cluttered with mail, condiments, and artificial sweetener packets.

I wasn't getting out of this conversation, at least not that easily.

The house had both a breakfast nook and a dining room. Except Gran wasn't the type of lady to own two dining tables. The dining room housed an assortment of cat trees, cat towers, scratching posts, and other furniture unsuitable for human rear ends. This little nook in the kitchen was where we ate our meals. *And now*, I thought, *it's where Gran goes crazy*.

She tapped her finger waiting for my reply, making the oversized ruby on her ring bounce. I wondered, not for the first time, if it was real.

"I'm not a witch," I said. "I think the word you're looking for starts with a B. And honestly, it's not a nice thing to call anyone, let alone your granddaughter."

Gran had made an occasional odd statement about witches or spells or curses. She told me to make a salt line beside my window to prevent bad dreams. When I arrived, she'd smelled me for curses, then explained it was me smelling of three days' travel.

But those were more easily brushed aside. This current bout of madness was proving more difficult.

"I know what I said, and I said what I meant. You're a witch, sweetheart. I thought you knew."

There she went again. Twice in as many minutes, calling me a witch. Or possibly the b-word.

The kettle whistled.

"Two sugars, and a squeeze of lemon, right?"

"Too right, dear."

I switched off the gas and set out our mugs.

"You *are* a witch," Gran said as I sat down. "Like me and like your mother. Here, I'll prove it to you."

"And just how are you going to do that?" I was getting

tired of this—and when I get tired, I get sarcastic. "Are you going to show me your wand? Or no, wait! I know. You'll twitch your little nose and make the table disappear. That's it! That'll show me! Go on then. Make the table disappear."

"Heavens, no," Gran scoffed. "Why would I want the table to disappear? This lack of magical knowledge, or surplus of fictional, only goes to show how much you've got to learn."

I sighed. "Okay. Then how *are* you going to prove it?"

"Stevie," Gran called. "Stevie, get in here. I need you."

Stevie, one of Gran's three housecats, rounded the corner into the kitchen. He leaped onto the table, purring madly in hopes Gran would stroke his back.

"Oh, you can stop that nonsense," she scolded him. "I've just told her."

The black shorthaired cat stopped purring. He chose instead to lick his paws. Then he gave his forehead a wash.

"Well, how did she take it?" The deep throaty voice of a man seemed to be coming from the area around the cat. To say it came from the cat's mouth would not be accurate. The voice was like a shadow without an owner.

I was shaken. Scared. I stumbled and landed on my backside, then scrambled away on the unswept kitchen floor. Grains of dirt dug into my palms as I scooted backward.

"That well." Gran pointed a gnarled finger in my direction.

My skull found a cabinet to bump against. "Ow!"

"And whose fault is that?" Gran asked. "Did either of us push you into the cabinet? For heaven's sake, Constance, I thought you'd take this better. You had to know something about you was different from everyone else."

"You thought I would take what better? Having a nervous breakdown?"

"You're not having a nervous breakdown."

"I beg to differ. I just heard a cat speak."

"Not exactly true," the cat's voice said.

"You see how well those movies prepared her," Gran said to the cat, to Stevie. "She can't even fathom a talking cat. Honestly, how good can they be?"

"I thought they were decent," Stevie replied. "Although it did get rather unbelievable toward the end."

"The magic?" Gran asked.

"No." He shook his cat head. "To believe those actors were only seventeen."

Stevie dropped to the floor and padded toward me. There was nowhere for me to go. Nowhere to run. He found my lap, placed his front paws on top of me, and stretched. His claws extended, piercing gently into my shirt.

"What do we have to do convince you?" his voice asked.

"To convince me what, that I'm a witch?"

"No," Stevie answered. "To convince you that this isn't a psychotic break. I know what you're thinking. And you're *not* crazy."

Gran leaned in my direction. "That's what you thought before, isn't it? When you stopped time. That you were crazy."

"How do you...? I, yeah, I feel a bit crazy."

Crazy and out of breath. The room was spinning. It was much easier to stay on the ground. Much, much easier.

Eventually I'll wake up, I thought, *and this will all have been a dream. A vivid and crazy dream.*

But I wasn't waking up. And those claws of his hurt.

"Okay," I said slowly, taking a breath. "Let's say I do

believe you. I'm a witch. You're a witch. You have a talking cat."

"A familiar."

"Right." I nodded. "I knew that." I knew what witches called their pets.

I got up shakily and returned to my seat. The tables had turned. Now it was me in need of that tea.

"My mom *was* a witch." The words stung leaving my lips. Since my mom died when I was so young, I was always learning new things about her, slowly building a picture of her in my mind. But this information made it seem like I'd been building a puzzle with half the pieces lost.

Gran pursed her lips, contemplative. "Constance, I've never gotten confirmation from the spirits that your mother *actually* did die. But being a witch is how she ended up wherever she is now. She took a job, a special assignment, and she never returned."

"But she had a job."

"No, no. She wasn't a... whatever you think she was." Gran shook her head.

"A studio location scout," I said. "Her plane went down in the Pacific. Dad told me this story a thousand..."

Gran took a sip of tea, unwilling to look me in the eyes.

"They never found the plane," I continued my spiel. And Gran continued to silently tell me it was wrong.

"So, there wasn't a plane crash?"

"It sounds like a *convenient* story to tell a gullible man."

I'd normally protest any word spoken against my father, but for now I held my tongue. A million questions buzzed around my head. Finding the right one to ask proved difficult.

"I thought maybe you'd have a few more questions," Gran said.

She was right. I had a ton, mostly to do with my mother and the circumstances around her—around her disappearance.

"Not about your mother," Gran said. "That's a subject for another time. Questions about being a witch. I'd assumed you might have a few."

"She does," Stevie's voice boomed. "Many more. I don't think she knows where to start."

"The simpler, the better," Gran said.

That narrowed the field. And it did make sense. With those words, I was able to find my first question.

"How do you know that I'm a witch?" I asked. "What if it skips a generation or something like that?"

"It doesn't. And you've already done some magic. Besides, we'll know soon enough. Your familiar will reveal itself on or before your fortieth birthday."

"My familiar." I nodded. "Are they always cats?"

Idly, I wondered why we didn't just share Stevie. Gran scooped him from the floor and put him on her lap.

He answered, "Not always. Your familiar could be anything. A dog, a cat, a mouse—any sort of rodent really. But let's hope it's not. These feline instincts, they aren't easy to hold back."

"Really?" I asked. "Anything?"

"The sky's the limit," Stevie said. "It could be a bird. Oh, I'd loathe it if it were a pigeon."

"Okay. Can I ask, what is a familiar exactly? Besides a pet. I get that. But were you once a human? I mean, I've seen that show, *Sabrina the Teenage Witch*. That's about all I've got to go on."

"Not human—never human," he answered. "No, we're fallen angels." Stevie's posture straightened. He could see the question on my lips. "Not demons. No. We are the neutrals in heaven's war. We didn't take a side, but we were cast out anyway, unwelcome in either realm. Neither heaven nor hell will take us."

"Ah. All right." I found my next question. "And why forty? Why not sixteen? Eighteen? Twenty-one?"

"If witches got their powers at sixteen, what do you think they'd use them on?" Gran had answered my question with a question of her own.

"To enslave humanity," Stevie guessed.

"No," Gran chortled. "Let Constance try. Think, child. What were *you* doing at eighteen—at twenty-one? Hell, at twenty-six you were already on what—marriage number two? Girls will be girls. And the younger they are, the—"

"Stupider," Stevie offered.

Gran grew more agitated. "That's not what I'm trying to say."

"I get it," I said. "Boys. We'd waste our magic on boys or something dumb." I felt compelled to defend myself. "But I wasn't married twice, Gran. Only the one time, to Mark."

"Honey," she said to me. "I don't care what the state says, once that Elvis impersonator said husband and wife, that's what you were."

It was a mistake. A weekend in Vegas. And a memory that I was happy to let *stay* in Vegas.

"Wait! How do you even know about that?" Gran knew a lot more about me than I knew about her.

She smiled. "I have my ways, my dear. And as I was saying, you're not a witch until you turn forty. In a few more days, I'll explain more. This weekend, to coincide with the full moon, we'll have a celebration in your honor."

"Like a party?"

She pursed her lips. "Like a party."

A party. For becoming a witch. I had so many more questions, but my mouth stayed closed, almost like Gran had spelled it shut.

She left me there in the kitchen to contemplate the craziness of the past half hour. Stevie pranced behind her, his tail up.

I heard her flick the television back on. Harry was learning to play quidditch.

5

IN WITCH I DISCOVER A DEAD BODY

In books, everyone is always plagued by bad dreams—especially when they're coming into their magic. But that night, I went to sleep as usual—by finding a podcast and listening to two people ramble until I passed out. I dreamed normal dreams with no witches, no demons or ghosts, nothing paranormal—nothing to indicate that in only a few days I'd become a witch with magical abilities of some sort. As of now, the list included stopping time and talking to cats. Or at least one cat.

I woke refreshed, as if the whole ordeal yesterday was actually the dream. Today was a day like any other. I was back in the ordinary world.

Then Stevie slinked into the room. "Feeling better?" His husky voice vibrated the chain on the ceiling fan.

"Not anymore," I said.

I left for work early, wanting out of the house. I needed to get away. Thoughts of California lingered in the back of my mind. I thought about putting my foot on the accelerator and not looking back.

Instead, I made sure to keep Crookshanks under the

speed limit. And I was at the grocery a good fifteen minutes before it opened—so early, in fact, that the front doors didn't slide open for me. I put my face up against the glass and banged hard to get someone's attention. No one came to my rescue.

I counted the cars in the parking lot.

"You've got to be kidding me."

There were two—Crookshanks and Mr. Caulfield's green Mustang.

I could wait for Trish, I thought. But neither of us had a key to the front of the store. So, if I wanted in, I'd have to go around back to the loading dock.

Just my luck. Late one day and too early the next. If only they evened out in Mr. Caulfield's eyes.

I edged around the building with my hands in my pockets. The back of the store had an industrial appearance, all concrete slab. A detached semi-trailer cast a long shadow toward the dumpster and recycling bin. Even from this distance, I could smell the funk of the trash. And either my mind was playing tricks on me, or I could hear rats squeaking.

The thought made me cringe. Heebie-jeebies sent a shiver down my spine. I was ready for a rat to streak across my path. But none did.

Behind the dumpster and off the pavement, past a dusty patch of sand, gravel, and weeds, the world turned into a tangled mess of woods. It was eerily dark. The orange loading dock light couldn't penetrate the dense foliage.

The shrill call of a screech owl sent me reeling. It made me feel like someone—or something—was watching me.

"*Hoo hoo hoo*," another owl replied.

This felt like the perfect time to meet my familiar. If so, it was definitely going to be a rat. Or maybe that owl. Either way, Stevie wasn't going to be thrilled.

But I made it to the door without incident.

The door opened with a strong push. I went from the darkness outside to the total darkness of the back room of the store. Only a single safety light was glowing. Somehow, this was worse than outside. Eerie.

"Hello?" I called. "Mr. Caulfield? Anyone?"

His office, which shared a wall with the breakroom, was also dark. I fumbled in my purse for my phone and switched on the flashlight function. Then I found the row of light switches beside the door. I flipped on the first. When it did nothing, I did the same for the second and third.

Finally, the fluorescent bulbs flickered to life. The breakroom and the office remained pitch black.

"Hello?" I said again, trying to make sure I was alone.

Mr. Caulfield must've left his car here overnight, I told myself.

Still, it was strange that no one else was here so close to opening. Granted, we weren't the type of grocery that had a bakery. Creel Creek had a bakery. Our stockers were done by ten every night. While I didn't appreciate Mr. Caulfield's attitude toward me, he did run a tight ship.

But where is he?

And did he really leave the doors unlocked?

I was at a crossroads. I could clock in. Get my till, count it, and be womanning my post before another soul got here. *Or, I can stand here awkwardly until another employee gets here.*

Back in California, I'd always liked getting to work early. It felt like the only time I could get things done. Sometimes, I'd work on the weekend—spend whole days alone in the office. I hadn't been scared off by a lack of people. No, I'd relished it.

So, why's this any different?

I made up my mind and sighed. *So what if I'm the only person here. So what if I'm not. And if Mr. Caulfield's lurking in the shadows, let him lurk.*

Okay, I didn't really want him to be lurking in the shadows. He was creepy enough already.

But in less than ten minutes, seven more people would be lining up with their timecards in hand. I got my vest and clocked in early. *Let's see if I get a reprimand for that.* All that was left was to get my till, from the safe in Mr. Caulfield's office.

He'd entrusted me with the code to the safe, but I wasn't allowed a key to the front door.

I guess it made sense, I'd need both to do any damage. And there wasn't much in the safe. Mr. Caulfield made trips to the bank twice a day. Plus, most people used cards now anyway, even in Creel Creek.

Besides, the real valuables were in the store proper, filling the milk case at almost five dollars a gallon. And in produce. In California, you could pick up avocados on any neighborhood street. Ours sold for almost three dollars.

I took a second to button my vest, then I reached inside Mr. Caulfield's office for the light switch. When the light came on, I saw that I'd been wrong. I wasn't the only person in the building. The office was occupied. Occupied by Mr. Caulfield.

Well, his cold lifeless body.

So, in another way, I was right—I was the only soul in the building.

The door behind me swung open.

6

THE VILLAGE VAMPIRE

"Early bird gets the worm," Trish chirped.

The door slammed shut behind her.

I was still at the doorway of Mr. Caulfield's office in a state of shock. My mind hadn't caught up to what my eyes were seeing. It was way worse than when I'd stopped time.

The scene wasn't gruesome, not in the traditional sense. There wasn't any blood that I could see.

Mr. Caulfield's body was splayed out in his desk chair, his arms dangling over the armrests. His eyes were wide open, staring up at the ceiling. He looked frozen—almost like he'd been locked in the walk-in freezer overnight and someone had put him in here to thaw.

"Honey," Trish said, "is everything okay?"

I shook my head vigorously.

I felt her presence behind me before she touched my shoulder and scooted me out of the way to see what was wrong. Then Trish grabbed me by both shoulders and pulled me away from the office.

"Take a few breaths, babe." I allowed her to guide me

into the breakroom. She pushed me into the closest chair. "You need to call 911. And you need to tell them to send the sheriff, not the city police. You got that?"

I stared up at her blankly. Her words didn't make sense. It took my brain far too long to parse them. Something about calling 911.

"Constance, did you touch anything?"

I shook my head.

"Good. Now, make that call." She grabbed my purse from my cubby and dug out my phone. With a reassuring squeeze, she put it in my hand. "Call," she said again. "I'll do what I can."

I dialed 911 for the first time in my life. I could hear my father's voice telling me to only use it in an emergency, a *real* emergency like I was eight years old again.

I guess this constituted a real emergency. Still, I couldn't dial.

Nevertheless, a voice spoke on the other end of the line. Calm. Immediate. "What is your emergency?"

I fumbled through the explanation, telling the operator about the body. She wanted me to make sure that Mr. Caulfield *was* dead. She wouldn't let me hang up the phone. I stood shakily and walked to Mr. Caulfield's office.

Trish was, well, she was doing something with her eyes closed. *Chanting?*

I couldn't make out the words. There was a pattern to them, a rhythm. She moved to the center of the office, waggling a finger in front of her. Spinning in a tight circle, she wiggled that finger in every direction. Next, she grasped at the air with both hands. At nothing. But for an instant, I saw something drop into her hands.

"Trish," I hissed, my own hand instinctively covering the

receiver. "What are you doing? They want to know if he's really dead."

She shook her head, indicating she wasn't going to deal with me.

"Miss? Hello?" The operator's voice was loud in my ear. "Is everything okay? Is he—can you confirm that he's deceased?"

"No," I said.

"No, he's not dead?"

"No," I repeated. "It's not okay. He's definitely dead."

Trish nodded in agreement but didn't stop murmuring and spinning. But she mouthed the word sheriff at me.

That's right.

"Sheriff Marsters," I said to the operator. "We need the sheriff." I hung up the phone and ignored it when they called me back. I couldn't stop looking at Mr. Caulfield. Not until Trish guided me away once again.

Nick and Hal came through the back door together. Trish waved them off, not allowing them to see inside Mr. Caulfield's office.

She put them on guard duty at the front of the store. "Let the police inside," she said. "No one else. We're closed today. All right?"

They nodded.

"Nick, it'd be good if you made a sign to put out by the road. I don't even want anyone in the parking lot. Use that big chalkboard over by the bananas."

"Will do." Nick gave her a mock salute.

"Should he really touch anything in the store?" I asked. "Couldn't it be evidence?"

Trish shook her head. "If they needed to dust every product for fingerprints, we'd be closed for months. There's no evidence out there."

"How do you know?" I asked her. Then I whispered so that only Trish could hear. "And do you know how he died?"

"That, I don't know," she said. "Sheriff Marsters will be here soon."

"You really think *he* can figure this out?" I didn't know much about small town law enforcement, but I didn't think the guy who pulled me over and couldn't give me a ticket should be investigating this—whatever this was. I don't know why, but my gut said it was murder.

"This has to be a murder."

"Just trust me," Trish said firmly.

"Trust you. Sure." I nodded, feeling my head come out of the clouds. It was still a long way to the ground. "How are you so—"

"Calm?" she suggested.

"Yeah..."

"Honey, I've always been good in emergencies. But usually, it's cuts or scrapes—or the time a customer needed CPR. Don't ask. Actually, the worst, before today, was a broken arm. My brother fell off the monkey bars when we were little kids."

"That's awful."

Trish stifled a smile. "Yeah. I was the one who pried his fingers loose."

I wanted to ask her what it was she'd been doing inside Mr. Caulfield's office, but then Terrance Stockton, a dairy associate, pushed open the door and stopped, his rotund shape filling the doorway. "I hear sirens," he announced.

"Good," Trish said, taking charge. "Go inside the breakroom and wait. Don't touch anything."

"Why?" he asked. "There been a crime or something?"

"Something like that."

I went with him, and we waited. After what felt like a

week but the clock said was two minutes, we heard a commotion at the front of the store.

A few seconds later, Sheriff Marsters pushed through the flapping two-way doors from the sales floor. A deputy, a woman, was trailing him. She had her pistol drawn, but it was pointing at the ground, and her finger wasn't on the trigger.

"There's no need for that," Trish said. "Whoever did this is long gone."

She thinks it's murder too, I thought.

"I'll be the judge of that," Sheriff Marsters said. He looked much the same as he had yesterday. The same bristly mustache and same five o'clock shadow—I guess it was five o'clock somewhere. Or maybe he was averse to shaving with an actual razor.

Trish gestured for them to look inside Mr. Caulfield's office.

They approached it with caution and looked inside. The female deputy holstered her weapon.

"All clear," the sheriff said into the radio on his shoulder. He took a deep breath, his eyes closed, and something about him changed. He shook his head like this didn't sit right. He sniffed the air. Then he went into full cop mode.

"Willow," he said to the deputy, "I want you to take a look around in there. Do your thing. Then I want you to herd everyone to the front of the store."

She nodded.

"And you two," he said to us. "You found the body?"

"She did." Trish pointed. What a traitor.

"Is that right, ma'am?"

I gave the meekest of nods. "I was here a minute—maybe two—before Trish got here." Two could play the blame game.

"All right. Let's find a place to chat." Sheriff Marsters, or just Dave, as he'd told me to call him, ushered me into the breakroom.

I expected him to close the door. Instead, he turned to Trish. "You coming?"

Reluctantly, she followed him in and he closed the door.

"Trish," he said, "do you mind putting on a pot of coffee?" The breakroom was equipped with an ancient coffee machine that brewed the most terrible sludge I've ever put in my mouth. I'd heard Trish flatly refuse to make coffee, telling both Nick and Hal that it wasn't her job.

This wasn't the time or the place for an argument. She got to work.

"You, sit." Just Dave pointed at the metal cafeteria-style table. It was cramped. I didn't like sitting there at lunch. And I especially didn't like sitting there now.

That was when the reality of the situation came crashing down. Someone was dead. He was never coming back. And odds were, someone had killed him.

My hands began to shake.

"It's okay." Dave crammed himself into the seat across from me. I hadn't realized how tall he was. He put his large hands around my large wrists. It did calm my nerves.

"Take a minute to collect yourself," he said. "You're okay. You're safe. I promise."

He waited.

Trish dropped a Styrofoam cup full of sludge next to him. It sloshed everywhere. Her silent protest. She leaned against the counter, not offering me anything.

"Let's start with some basics. Your name is Constance, right?"

"Right."

"Your license was from California, I believe. I was

being nice yesterday. The state says you're supposed to transfer your license. But a new license is the last thing on anyone's mind when they're moving. Can you tell me how long you've lived here? How long you've worked at the grocery. And can you tell me where you live—your new address?"

I told him everything he wanted to know, including Gran's address.

"Wait—" He made a face. "You live with Jezebel Young?"

"That's right. I'm her granddaughter."

The sheriff shot Trish a questioning look, asking without words if she was privy to this information. She was, I knew, because Trish was the one who'd helped Gran get me this job.

Trish nodded.

"Oh, well then, maybe you can help us."

I didn't know what he meant. I thought I *was* helping. I was doing the best I could. I didn't know anything, only that I'd found a body.

I wondered why I was supposed to help when I was the victim here. Okay, not *the* victim. But I'd been through an ordeal. I found a dead body.

"I'm not sure what you mean," I said. "Aren't you the sheriff?"

"I am," he said. "But I thought—well, I thought—"

"He thought you were a witch," Trish interjected.

Yesterday's conversation with Gran—the assertion that I was a witch—had been overshadowed by the morning's events. For a moment, I wondered if Gran had told them. *Does the whole town know? And why are they bringing it up?*

"Exactly that," Dave confirmed.

"She's not of age," Trish explained, annoyed. "Not yet."

The sheriff looked me up and down, probably thinking

how much I did look *of age*. I hadn't been carded to buy alcohol in years.

"How old are you, Miss Campbell?"

"I turn forty on Sunday."

He raised his eyebrows at Trish as if confirming forty was the *magic* number.

She nodded, again annoyed. Maybe they'd had this conversation before.

"Sorry," he said. "I never can remember the finer points with you lot. You can't be simple like the rest of us. Not that mixing puberty with 'the change'"—he made air quotes—"is easy. Far from it."

I wasn't following. He could tell and clarified, "I've got three pups at home."

"Pups?" I was even more confused.

"Dave's a werewolf," Trish said.

"A werewolf," I repeated slowly. "You've got to be kidding."

They didn't understand that not only was this stuff new to me, it also sounded like a joke. It shouldn't be real. Gran had *just* told me the witch part. Now, they were adding werewolves to the craziness?

"And if you're wondering what this has to do with what you saw in there—" Sheriff Marsters hooked his thumb at the office. "Well, Eric—that is, Mr. Caulfield, was Creel Creek's resident vampire."

"We have a resident vampire?"

"*Had* a resident vampire," the sheriff corrected.

"Among other things," Trish added. "Willow, the deputy over there, she's a psychic. And like you and your grandmother, I'm a witch." She shrugged nonchalantly. "I wanted to tell you."

I wanted to tell her that there was no definitive proof

that I actually was a witch. Except this didn't feel like a sympathetic crowd.

Dave spoke up for me. "She's not a witch. Not yet. Remember? As of now, she's a witness and nothing more."

"I'm not even that," I objected. "I didn't see anything. Except for his body."

"Weird, isn't it?" Dave said. "I've never seen anything like that."

"You think I have?"

"I'd guess not." He returned his attention to Trish. "Well, do *you* have anything for me? I won't know much until the medical examiner gets here. And you know how *he* can be."

"I do." Trish winced. "I hate to tell you, but there wasn't much in his office. Only a word."

"That's it?" Dave questioned. "A word. What word?"

"Daylight," Trish said softly.

7

BEWITCHED BOOKS

When they let us leave the scene, I thought the ordeal was over. Done with—at least for the day. But the parking lot had turned into a zoo. And not with people who wanted to buy groceries.

No one respects a chalkboard sign.

The lot was filled with rubberneckers. This was the worst of small-town America.

In California, there was hardly a time I couldn't hear a siren. And it was only during those times, when the eerie silence filled my ears, that I thought something bad might actually be happening—a spaceship hovering in the sky. Russia launching their nuclear arsenal.

The rare siren in Creel Creek had called the locals from their hovels. Among them, a red-haired woman with a face like a duck and a microphone in her hand. The news van had parked close to the police barricades.

The reporter perked up when she saw us and she trotted over. Her dumpy and disheveled cameraman hustled behind her, a camera on his out-of-shape shoulders.

"Who's she?" I whispered to Trish.

"Summer Shields. Local reporter. *Live on the scene*," Trish mocked. "Don't tell her anything. Ever, if you can manage."

Summer thrust her microphone in Nick's direction, but the produce manager shook her off. She skipped Hal, who seemed keen to talk with her. She shoved her microphone in Trish's face instead. Trish pushed the microphone away. "I don't think so."

I was really starting to like Trish.

Undeterred, the reporter whipped the microphone in my direction.

"Ma'am," she said, "do you work here? Can you tell our viewers what happened today? We understand there was a death."

"Listening to the police scanner again, Summer?" Trish asked.

The reporter paid her no mind, her eyes and her microphone remained fixed on me.

"It was the manager, Eric Caulfield, wasn't it? Our viewers want to know."

"Your viewers are all here in the parking lot with you," Trish pointed out.

This time Summer wasn't so professional. "You had your chance for the spotlight. You can shove it, Trish."

"Oh, I don't think you'd like where I'd shove it," Trish retorted.

Summer jabbed the microphone closer. I could take a bite out of it. "Ma'am, can you describe the scene? What's it like in there? Were you the one who discovered the body?"

"I, uh—" She sensed my weakness—my reluctance to lie.

"And was it Eric Caulfield, the manager? Creel Creek wants to know." This girl wasn't letting up. She was going in for the kill. "Viewers, they want the picture painted for them."

Trish intervened. "Sorry, Summer. We didn't bring our paints. Come on, Constance, let's go." She took my arm again and gently pulled me away.

"Oh, it's going to be like that, is it?" Summer asked her. "You know, most people like being on TV. They like being famous. Your friend here might want a few minutes in the limelight."

"She doesn't," Trish said. "You're the only one who wants to be famous."

"That's enough for now." Sheriff Marsters stepped up to the barricade. "Give me a minute, and I'll give you a brief statement. Is that good enough, Ms. Shields?"

"I guess so," Summer Shields conceded.

Trish led me through the parking lot to Mr. Caulfield's Mustang. We waited there while the crowd gathered around the sheriff.

He outlined the situation, leaving out the word murder and much of what the three of us had discussed inside. There was no mention of werewolves, vampires, or witches. Finally, he said, "Caulfield Grocery is closed indefinitely."

"Where are we supposed to get groceries?" a man in the crowd asked.

"Yeah, cause you're here for groceries, Hank," the sheriff scoffed. "I don't care where you get them. Hidden Creek's not too far. Or go to Lynchburg or Charlottesville. If you don't want to drive, the Circle Q's been serving me breakfast for almost twenty years. They've got milk and some produce."

That caused a disgruntled murmur.

"Let's get out of here," Trish said in my ear.

"No," I declined. "I've got to—"

"Come on." She wasn't taking no for an answer. And the truth was, I had nowhere to be. Gran wouldn't be missing me for several hours, unless Summer's coverage cut into *The Price Is Right*.

"Fine."

Trish had parked right next to Mr. Caulfield. Reluctantly, I got into her car, a beat-up Volkswagen with a diesel engine that sputtered to life with a thick cloud of black smoke.

Trish drove toward downtown Creel Creek, turning onto Main Street.

I wish I could say that this part of town was quaint and charming—or any of those other things that people usually associate with small towns. I wish it was revitalized and bustling. But it's none of those things.

The only thing interesting on the main thoroughfare was the charred shell of what was once the Creek County Courthouse, sixty years ago. After the fire, the county decided to move both the courthouse and the county seat twenty miles east, to Hidden Springs.

Trish angle-parked outside a row of storefronts, all of which were empty save a used bookstore, Bewitched Books, and a smoke shop.

I hoped she wasn't going for a pack of cigarettes or one of those vape pens. But she went to the bookstore and unlocked the front door.

"Wait. You work here too?"

"I don't work here. I own it." Trish flipped the sign in the front window from CLOSED to OPEN. "It used to be my mom's shop. Now it's mine."

"If you own this place, why do you work at the grocery store?"

"You're joking, right?" Trish scoffed. "Look around. People don't shop in used bookstores anymore. I'm lucky if this place makes enough to cover the rent. And the rent isn't much. You see the competition."

There was no competition.

"It's still cool," I said. "You grew up in a bookstore."

"Like I said, a *used* bookstore," she said as if the word itself was tainted. "And it's mostly specialty used books at that."

She was wrong. It was cool that she grew up in a bookstore. Even a dim, drab, and dusty bookstore was heaven in my mind. Her shop was redolent with the scent of old books, faintly musty but with a sweet undertone.

Like her, I'd grown up with books. Only for me, they'd been an escape. An escape from the fact that my mom was never coming back, that it was just me and my dad—who was also someone who always had a book in his hand.

This place reminded me of the bookstores hidden around San Francisco. The small shops where the coffee was only adequate, but the conversations were the best in town.

Here there were shelves for romance, mystery, and science fiction. But Trish hadn't been kidding. More than half of the space was devoted to the supernatural—books on the occult, of pagan rituals, and Wiccan magic.

"We have a few regulars," Trish said. "Your grandmother is one of them. But mostly this store survives by being an Amazon seller. I ship these books around the world. Books on magic—*real* magic—they're hard to find. And I specialize in finding them. Or rather, Mom did."

"How?" I asked.

"A spell. Essentially, when a spell book loses its owner, it finds its way here. I can't even explain it myself."

"Is that like what you did this morning?"

"Sort of. That was a summoning spell too. I can teach you how to do one if you like."

"Sure," I said without meaning it. Then something else clicked. "If it's that easy, why couldn't you just summon the murderer or their name or whatever? Like why can't you just say 'Who killed Mr. Caulfield?'"

"For one, it doesn't rhyme. And two, it's not that easy. Summoning spells have to be precise. *Extremely* precise. They either won't work or they'll blow up in your face."

"That doesn't make any sense," I said.

"Magic doesn't make a whole lot of sense." Trish shrugged. "Think about it. Death is inevitable. We're all going to die, eventually. And another thing, is it the knife or the murderer that really kills a person? What makes this death even more complex is that our victim was technically already dead."

"That's true?" I asked her. "About vampires, I mean. That they're dead."

"In most senses of the word, yes." She clarified, "But not all. Here, I have a book for you. We'll call it an early birthday present. It'll help you figure out some of this witch stuff."

"No, you don't have to do that," I said. "Or at least let me pay for it."

"Definitely not."

"Why not?"

She shook her head. "Listen. I've been rude to you since the day we met. I'm sorry about that, by the way. It's just, since my mother died, well, your Gran, she's been—she's been really kind to me. When you got here, I sort of felt like you were on my territory. But it wasn't even mine to begin with. She's *your* grandmother. And I didn't realize how complicated your situation really was. Now, if I can find that book... Give me a second."

She perused the center aisle and came back with a thin book. It wasn't exactly the grimoire or the spell book I expected.

"Sorry, what do you mean, *my* situation?" I asked her.

"I mean, you didn't even know you were a witch. At least I don't think you did. Not until—"

"Yesterday."

"That's what I thought. That's insane. I knew I was a witch, or that I was going to be a witch, since I was five, I think. I had to wait thirty-five years to get my powers. And when I did, two years ago, my mother wasn't here to help me learn to use them. I guess we have that in common."

"What happened to your mom?" I asked.

"My dad happened."

"He found out she was a witch?"

"If only it was that simple." Trish sighed. "Maybe you've figured it out by now, but things around Creel Creek aren't exactly normal. See, he—my husband—was a wielder of magick too. The kind with a K at the end. It's an important distinction."

She saw I wasn't following, rolled her eyes, and said, "It'll be in the book. The book explains it much better than I can."

"They always do."

She handed it to me. *So, I Guess You're A Witch* looked like it was meant for girls in elementary school.

Trish continued her story. "Warlocks aren't like us. Our magic comes from the Earth. From the spirit."

"And theirs?"

"Read the book," she said. "Okay. Fine. Some say that long ago a magician made a deal with the devil, trading his soul for power. I don't exactly buy that. But I do think their power comes from death.

"My father killed my mother. He stole her powers. He probably would've done the same to me eventually, had Willow not seen it in a vision and Sheriff Marsters not acted in time. I owe them both my life."

"It sounds like it," I said. "What about your brother? Is he warlock too?"

She smiled. "No. He's the smart one in the family. My brother made something of himself. He lives in Florida with three kids and a non-witch wife. He left all of this behind. He doesn't want power."

"Speaking of powers," I said, changing the subject, if only a little. "Willow—I mean Deputy Brown—how do *her* powers work?"

"Call her Willow. Call Dave, Dave. Trust me, they'll be mad at you if you don't. I *think* it's like being a witch, except Willow can't really control her visions. That doesn't stop her from trying, but they just happen. She tried hard today, I'm sure."

"And we can control our powers." It was phrased as a statement, one I hoped was correct.

Trish sighed. "Sort of. Every witch's powers are different. Some are better at divination than others. It's not really *my* strong suit."

"What is?"

"Read the book! You'll figure it out."

"How is the book going to—"

"Stop being stubborn and read it. You're worse than—"

A rustling from behind her caused me to jump. A mouse scurried around a stack of books. Instinctively, I looked for the closest broom. There wasn't one.

Calmly, Trish reached down and scooped up the mouse with both hands. She cradled it to her chest.

Then I realized it must be Trish's familiar. The mouse was huffing and puffing. It had to be the fattest mouse I'd ever seen. Not that I hung around many mice.

"It's just Twinkie," Trish said. "He hates to be left out."

"Crossing the store never gets any easier, ya know," the deep growl of a familiar chided her. "And I was trying to figure out what you were doing here so early. And talking witchy business on top of that."

"This is Constance," Trish told him.

"Ah, yes. I've heard a lot about you."

"That not true," Trish denied. "I've hardly said a thing. Your grandmother is tightlipped. She's only mentioned you and your mother a few times in passing."

"Up until yesterday, I thought my mother died in a plane crash."

"And now?"

"I don't even know if she's dead."

Trish shook her head. "Wow."

She moved Twinkie to her shoulder. At first, I'd thought he was a white mouse, a lab mouse, but now I realized his fur was mostly gray with sprinkles of light brown and black. His eyes were black and beady.

"Is Twinkie a boy or a girl's name?" I asked.

"Technically, a familiar is neither," Trish said.

"And technically my mouse parts are female," Twinkie's voice reverberated through the room.

"Fine then," Trish said. "*She* was my mother's familiar. And she stuck around after Mom died. We didn't have to go through that awkward stage, if you will."

"The awkward stage?"

"You know, like what's going on with us right now.

Becoming friends. Getting to know each other's habits. All that jazz."

Trish was right. We *were* becoming friends. *How weird.*

"Why are you looking at me like that?" she asked.

"Oh," I said, startled. "No reason."

But the harsh reality was, I didn't need a new friend right now. I needed to not be a witch. I needed not to have found a dead vampire. It was time I made my way back to California and put all of this crazy stuff behind me.

8

IN WITCH WE MEET SOMEONE NEW

"I guess I'll take you back to your car." Trish scooped her keys off of the counter and stowed Twinkie in her cleavage. "You good for a ride, little one?"

"I hate it when you put me here," she said.

"She says that, but I'm not sure it's true." Trish winked.

I held up the book. "I really do want to pay for it." Paying for it would ease my conscience.

Especially, I thought, *when I leave this place in my dust*.

After this morning, I was ready to point Crookshanks at California and stomp on the gas. Witch or not, I didn't like being around a murderer—especially one who could off an undead vampire.

Trish ignored me. "By now," she said, "I bet the parking lot's cleared out. Even if the sheriff's still there."

"Do you think he will be?"

Trish studied me. It was a casual question, one with no subtext. Still, it was like she was looking into me.

"You like him, don't you?" She pushed some loose strands of purple hair back, and with a dramatic hand to her forehead, squeaked, "Oh, Sheriff, I'd love to go in for an interrogation."

"Stop. No, I wouldn't."

The front door jingled.

I pivoted and found a man standing in the doorway. He seemed hesitant to step into the shop until his dark eyes met mine. He smiled.

His looks were a stark contrast to the rough-around-the-edges sheriff—who I totally didn't have a crush on. This man had the dreamy looks of a movie star—a clean-shaven face with strong features, a cleft in his chin, and cheekbones most women would kill for. His wavy dark hair was so thick it'd stop your fingers if you ran them through it. He chose a brushed back style, not too messy, not too neat. He was slim but filled out his button-down shirt. A button-down shirt with the top two buttons undone.

He smiled. "Mornin', ladies."

"It *is* morning," Trish conceded. "Did you read the sign on the door? We're not *supposed* to be open for a couple of hours."

"I did," he admitted. "Then I used my powers of observation. People inside. An unlocked door. The open sign."

"Crap," Trish muttered under her breath. "We're only here because—"

"Because of what happened up at the grocery store?" he guessed.

"How'd you—"

"TV." He shrugged nonchalantly. "That redheaded reporter is cute. You were in the video, you know?"

He pointed at me, losing some handsome points by calling the duck-faced Summer Shields cute.

Plus, the more I looked at his hair, the more I thought he

was showing off. *Hey, I'm over thirty and I don't have a receding hairline.*

"All right," Trish said. "You got me. How can I help you today?"

"I'm looking for a book. So, I thought I'd swing by."

"Did you try Amazon?" Trish asked.

"Why would I try there? I want it today."

"Two-day shipping. Or it could be an e-book. You could be reading it on your phone right this minute." Trish brushed at her chest. Twinkie had tried to sneak a peek.

"No." He shook his head. "I don't want to read it on my phone. Are you really trying to turn away a customer? Does your boss know you treat people like this?"

"I'm not turning you away," Trish argued. "You'd know if I was."

She totally *was* turning him away.

"And what *I* do with *my* business is *my* business. I'm my own boss."

"You really are the friendly sort."

"As friendly as they come," Trish retorted.

"I'm Cyrus—or Cy—by the way. And you are?" He was asking me, not Trish.

"I'm, uh—"

"She's not interested."

This was the third time Trish had come to my rescue in two days. The first time with Hal, I should've let her. The second time, with Summer, I gladly accepted. This time, I was somewhere in the middle.

"Wow. You two know how to make the new guy in town feel welcome." This time, he smiled enough to reveal a set of dimples. He got a few handsome points back.

"You're new in town?" I couldn't help myself. New to

town like me, and in a place as small as Creel Creek. *What an odd coincidence.*

Trish thought so too. “What, did they start incentivizing?” she scoffed.

Cyrus chuckled.

“I’m serious. Did you two get checks in the mail or something? She”—Trish pointed at me—“just moved here a few weeks ago.”

“I did,” I agreed. “They said my check’s in the mail.”

“It’s a small check,” Cyrus said. “Very small. I got mine yesterday.” The dimples returned, but I was over it. I was *not* getting involved with anyone who’d voluntarily move to Creel Creek, Virginia.

“No, but seriously,” he said, “I live here now. My father left me the vineyard outside of town.”

“Your father was Mr. Armand?” Trish asked.

“He was.” Cyrus nodded.

“But you never lived here,” Trish said pointedly. It wasn’t a question.

“No, no. I was raised by my mother, overseas—in Egypt, in France, and Belgium. I did spend holidays here every now and again. It feels like ages ago.”

Honestly, I’d thought the vineyard was closed. I’d seen it from the road, running errands for Gran. It looked abandoned. Maybe it was and Cyrus was going to revamp the place.

But those were questions I could ask Trish later. Her annoyance at his presence escalated when she found out who he was.

“I really am here for a book,” he told her.

“I’m sure you are,” Trish said. “Well, feel free to take a look around. I guess we’re open.”

Cyrus began to comb the shelves until Trish realized her

mistake. She wasn't admitting defeat, not exactly, but she wanted this guy out of her shop as soon as possible.

"What book is it?"

"*The Ghostly Guide to Astral Projections*. You heard of it?"

"It sounds vaguely familiar," Trish sighed. "Try the first aisle, toward the back on the right."

Any attraction was lost at this point. I might soon be a witch, but I was never going to be into a guy who believed in ghosts.

Trish must've had similar feelings. "So, you're into ghosts?" she called to him.

We could no longer see him; two shelves of books blocked our view.

"Maybe I'm a ghost hunter," he said.

He found the book and strode to the counter, pleased with himself. "There. I knew you'd have it."

"Are you *really* a ghost hunter?" I asked speculatively.

"Maybe."

Trish rolled her eyes, but he caught her in the act. "What? You mean to say you sell this stuff and you don't *believe* in it?"

"I'm cautiously pessimistic," Trish replied. "I've seen a few things, but nothing definitive. And I'm even less confident you're a ghost hunter. You're too pretty."

"That might be true." Yep, he was severely conceited. "But there's a lot going on in this town." He looked at me. "You should do yourself a favor and learn more about it. The check's only good if you stay around for a while."

He paid for the book. It was a little more expensive than the average used book. Okay, it was a lot more expensive. Almost twenty dollars.

"It was nice meeting you two," he said, not meaning it.

"We didn't meet," I replied. "Meeting requires the exchange of names."

"Oh, but we did," he countered. "I'm Cyrus, like I said. And you're Constance Campbell. I remember from the TV. Her name is Trish Harris. It's on these business cards." He pointed to the cards beside the register.

"That's not the same," I argued. "Plus, we don't even know your last name. Is it Armand like the vineyard?"

"Go ahead," he told Trish. "Tell her who I am."

"Cyrus Tadros," Trish said with contempt. "Son of Edward Armand, I guess."

"Mother never liked his last name," Cyrus said. "See, I saw you scrutinize my credit card. You really need to get one of those fancy readers like they have at the bakery. The ones that read chips and let me sign with my finger."

"Buy a few more books and maybe I can afford one," Trish retorted.

"Maybe," Cyrus wavered. "But not today. Like I said, it was nice meeting you two. Don't get into too much trouble, now."

With that, he left the shop.

I waited one second before laying into Trish. "What was that about?"

"It's not what you think," Trish said. "I mean it might be —what do you think?"

"Honestly, I don't know," I admitted. "I thought you two might know each other. You came off kind of…"

"Rude," Trish suggested.

"Something like that." I was actually thinking of the word I'd thought Gran had mistaken for witch.

"No wonder this place has trouble covering the rent," I said.

Trish shook her head. "I don't know who he is. But in the

few years I've run this place, we've *never* had a new customer. Not one that wasn't online. I don't know what his agenda is, but I'm confident he has one."

"So, you don't think he's a ghost hunter?"

Trish shook an imaginary Magic 8-Ball. "All signs point to no."

"And his father? Who is he? Or who was he?"

"That's another thing," Trish said. "I didn't know he had died. The vineyard's been there for as long as I can remember."

"You mean it's still a vineyard? It looks closed." I was surprised by that.

"That's cause it *is* closed," Trish said. "At least, it's closed to visitors. But they still produce wine. Good wine, too. I might have a bottle at home."

"So, what's his agenda, then?" I asked.

"I'm not sure. But I'm thinking maybe it has something to do with Mr. Caulfield's death."

9

TOO FAMILIAR

After Trish dropped me off at my car, I returned to Gran's. Gran and her familiar were dying for the inside scoop, Stevie more so than Gran. He hovered on the fringes of the conversation, not saying much. I think he realized it unsettled me.

How am I ever going to get used to a familiar? I didn't think I wanted or needed one.

"This is all my fault," Gran muttered.

"What is?"

"Your involvement," she said. "I knew that vampire was trouble. But I never would've believed something like this could happen. Not here. Not now. I shouldn't've summoned you here."

What happened next was like when I'd stopped time, except Gran was still talking—well, her mouth was moving. I'd actually hit the mute button. When she realized there was no sound coming out, she looked puzzled.

I shook my head. "You just said you summoned me."

"I never said that," she lied, her voice coming back. "I mean, I shouldn't have said that." Gran looked sheepish.

I gaped at her, dumbstruck. This made so much sense. When I'd gotten into the car, I was heading for my dad's place in San Diego. Gran used magic to get me here.

"I had to," she pleaded. "You were never going to learn anything out there on your own. When your husband did what he did, it made things a whole lot easier."

I couldn't hide how much that upset me. It explained everything. The problem was, I was here now. And though I was ready to pack up and leave, I didn't think the sheriff would appreciate it. There was also the coming into my powers thing to deal with—she did have a point there. A small one.

"You're terrible," I said.

I locked myself in my room for a few hours in my best reenactment of a teenage tantrum. *Forty going on fourteen.*

Before I got here, Gran had used her spare room to stow her sewing supplies—not that she was much of a seamstress, she was more of a collector of sewing materials.

There were yards and yards of fabric packed tightly on a bookshelf beside an old Singer sewing machine. It lived under a blanket of dust on a desk barely big enough to hold it.

Above the fabric, I'd cleared space to house my small collection of books. I put the one from Trish next to my copy of *The Tales of Beedle the Bard*. Strange, how so much of my life's reading centered around magic and the paranormal, almost as if I'd sought it unknowingly. Now, I wanted to push magic away.

This small collection was all I had kept from a lifetime of reading. Over the years, I'd given books to friends, donated them, and even left a whole bookcase at the house with Mark.

It doesn't matter, I thought. I can find almost everything on digital these days. Trish even asked that Cyrus guy why he hadn't looked for his book online.

But are Trish's suspicions justified? Could he really be the killer?

If being new in town meant getting labeled a murderer, then what was I, suspect number two?

And how do you kill a vampire, anyway?

Gran didn't know how it worked. She didn't know much about Mr. Caulfield, except that he was a vampire—information I could've used yesterday and the days before it.

Then again, I thought, *maybe "vampire" is just a label. Someone who drinks blood. But whose blood?*

I hadn't been brave enough to ask if they lived forever or could turn into bats. Gran said my knowledge about witches was wrong. Perhaps the same was true about vampires.

I glared at my frayed copy of *Twilight.*

How dare you forsake me.

One thing was certain, Vampires don't sparkle. Mr. Caulfield wasn't ghostly white either, not even redhead pale. And he wasn't beautiful by any stretch of the word.

I flopped onto the bed where I hoped to achieve an afternoon nap, but my racing mind wouldn't allow it. I went to the bookshelf again.

Despite my animus of all things witchy, I leafed through Trish's book. It read like bad fanfiction, like a book of wannabe nursery rhymes. And like all nursery rhymes, it dealt with death and the macabre—and of witches' trials and tribulations.

The first was about a witch that was convinced another witch was hexing her dairy cows so they wouldn't produce as much milk. The next verse, she claimed a wizard had taken the form of a goat to spy on her. She was careful not to let the goat see her true powers, afraid that the wizard would attempt to steal them.

Eventually she did, by accident. And when her suspicions proved to be true—the wizard tried to kill her—the other witch, the one she thought hexed her cows, killed him.

I guessed the moral of the story was to trust your fellow witches but be wary of wizards.

Judging by my chat with Trish earlier, she's taken this advice to heart.

It was midafternoon when I looked up from the book. Time had gotten away from me. I would have sworn I'd only been reading a few minutes or so.

My stomach growled, and I realized I hadn't eaten lunch.

I made a quick sandwich and spent the afternoon and evening steering clear of my grandmother and her familiar. Tough, considering they hung around in the places I wanted to be—the living room and the kitchen, respectively.

I wandered outside to the garden. Not that I felt like gardening, I just wasn't ready to talk to Gran again. I was bound to say something not nice. I wanted to be left alone. But an icy prickling sensation told me that it wasn't going to happen.

Someone—or rather, something—was watching me.

In the excitement of the morning, I'd completely forgotten about finding my familiar.

The sun had already dipped behind the mountains; only a sliver remained. And the wood between the cemetery and Gran's fenceless garden filtered those rays into almost nothing.

It grew darker the closer I got to the edge of the yard. I stopped several feet away from the trees, giving myself a wide berth if I needed to run.

"Hello?" I said tentatively, hoping that whatever it was would show itself.

I scoured the tree line for movement.

I was beginning to get frustrated by the lack of initiative on my familiar's part. If whatever, *whoever*, it was is supposed to be my familiar, why hadn't they showed their face?

An owl hooted.

"A bit early for you to be out," I called to it.

It didn't reply.

I gave up and turned toward the house, checking over my shoulder a couple of times. I climbed up the steps to Gran's deck and discovered a pair of yellow eyes I was sure were responsible for that prickly sensation.

"Why were you watching me?" I asked.

"You can't refuse the call forever, you know?" Stevie didn't bother answering my question. His gravelly voice was like nails in a woodchipper.

"I'm not refusing any call," I replied. "In fact, I was out looking for my familiar. No one was there. Except an owl."

"You know I can read your thoughts, right?" Stevie said.

I almost fell down the steps. "I, uh, no... I didn't."

Stevie didn't smile—cats don't do that—but I could tell he was smiling inwardly.

"Your familiar won't present itself until you're ready. Truly ready. Your mind and your heart have to be aligned."

Oh. While I wanted my familiar to go ahead and show itself, I wasn't ready. I wasn't ready to be a witch. After today's events, after Gran's confession, I didn't think I wanted to be.

"Can you really read my mind?" I asked him.

"Yes."

But can you really, I thought.

"Yes," he said.

"Never do that again."

I was struck by an awful thought.

Can other things read minds?

"You'll have to be more specific." Again, Stevie had eavesdropped on my thoughts.

"Can a vampire?" I asked.

"I believe so."

"I knew it." I'd known there was something odd about Mr. Caulfield. He said I'd been snippy. I felt violated.

But how do you kill a man who can read your mind?

Stevie licked a paw.

"What? No opinion for a change?"

"Sorry," he said. "I got bored. What are we talking about?"

"About Mr. Caulfield's murder," I said exasperatedly. "How would someone pull that off if he could read their thoughts?"

Stevie considered. "I think it would take someone highly intelligent. They'd need to be skilled at—"

"Occlumency," I interrupted him. Finally, my Harry Potter knowledge was going to be useful.

"At keeping their thoughts to themselves," Stevie countered. "There's no such thing as that nonsense from your movies."

"They're books."

"It's simple really," Stevie said. "All it takes is not thinking a thought in the vampire's presence. Give him no reason to suspect you and he won't."

"That sounds simple enough," I admitted.

"Still," Stevie said as he stretched, "a six-hundred-year-old vampire has other means of protecting himself. And your culprit defeated those as well."

Stevie headed for the cat door with his tail high. He left me there to stew.

Inside, there was spaghetti—a strainer full of clumped noodles and some reheated sauce with ground turkey. Gran passed this off as cooking.

I went inside, but now she was nowhere to be found. It wasn't just me steering clear of her. She was avoiding me too.

I fell into bed, the day weighing on me. Still, I was too wired to get to sleep. It was time to find another podcast. I decided to take Cyrus's advice to heart and learn more about Creel Creek. So I found one. A podcast that was oddly specific and local. But based on its reviews, it was odd. Something too fantastic to be real.

10

CREEL CREEK AFTER DARK, EPISODE 44

IT'S GETTING LATE.

Very late.
The creeping dread of tomorrow haunts your dreams.
It's dark out. Are you afraid?
Welcome to Creel Creek After Dark.

Athena: I'm your host, Athena Hunter.

Ivana: And I'm the lovely Ivana Steak.

Athena: So lovely.

Ivana: As are you, my dear.

Athena: You're too kind. You think we should start the episode?

Ivana: I think so.

Athena: Good. Cause I already started recording. This week has been quiet, hasn't it?

Ivana: It has. That's why this episode is a little out of the norm for us.

Athena: But we return to normal programming next week with a very special episode. That's right. We're finally doing it. The vineyard episode. Are you excited to record it?

Ivana: I am. A little nervous, though. For those who

don't know, we record these shows about a week in advance. And we're recording next week's episode tomorrow.

Athena: It's going to be fun. Anyway, what'd you say was on the playbill today?

Ivana: Today, we're reading a story sent in by one of our listeners.

Athena: And not just any story. This is a true story.

Ivana: So we're told.

Athena: Right, so we're told. And it's set right here in Creel Creek—Virginia's *spookiest* town.

Athena: What do you think about it, Ivana? It's about a witch.

Ivana: I think it could be true. We've heard rumors of a group of women who meet in the old graveyard. Granted, I heard it from the same person who claims to have seen a wolf twice the size of a man in his backyard.

Athena: Our listeners will remember episode thirteen, where we explored the graveyard's history, dating back to a mine explosion in the early 1800s.

Ivana: But was it really a mine explosion?

Athena: That tends to be the question we ask.

Ivana: So, without further ado. Here's *The Cabin,* author unknown.

A WITCH LIVED in a cabin in a wood, just past the end of a dirt road on the outskirts of Creel Creek, Virginia.

The fact was that the road wasn't actually a road, but the drive to the cabin is of little consequence. The fact that no persons living in said town had ever seen the witch drive a car is also of little consequence.

What is, however, of consequence, is the fact that she

lived alone. She rarely ventured out. And when she did, her interactions were few and far between.

Ten minutes after such an event, the interactees—the people that did meet the witch—a cashier at the grocery, a man at the post office, the farmer selling apples beside the road, well, they could hardly remember a thing about her. Whether she was five feet tall or six feet. Whether she had red hair or gray. Whether she had a long and bulbous nose, pinkish at the end, or no nose whatsoever.

It was the former—it's *always* the former.

The witch was a short woman with fiery red hair. She dyed it with beet juice. And she had a rather long nose that blossomed into a plum-sized knob at the end. Her eyes were yellow. They had no problem seeing in darkness, which is how on this particular night, the witch knew she wasn't alone in her cabin.

Now, her living space, if you can call it that, was a cluttered area with an abundance of old boxes. A shelf or two of herbs hung next to the fireplace where a cauldron waited. The witch had no need for wood or kindling.

On the opposite side of the room, there were two rows of cages. Some were empty. Most were occupied. Occupied by what, you might ask. Well, there was a possum, at least two squirrels, three snakes, and a hawk.

The witch had nothing to fear from the animals, not while they were locked away. It was the human skulking about that bothered her.

This human was briefly put off by the hissing, the clawing and the scratching, and the hoot of the owl. To the witch, these were ordinary sounds—nothing to worry over.

"I see you," the witch whispered into the darkness.

The intruder wasn't surprised by the witch's words. They didn't reply. Only their hand moved, pulling a dagger from some concealment on their person. Its blade glinted, caught by a sliver of moonlight.

"I knew you'd come back," the witch said.

"I'm not here to kill you," the intruder said. "I'm here for the book. Killing you is just a perk. Now, where is it?"

"You'll never find it."

"I'll make you suffer before you die." It wasn't an empty threat. The intruder was going to make the witch suffer no matter the outcome of the book search.

"I've suffered enough these last few years." There was no strain in the witch's voice. No pleading. "And I don't plan to do any more at *your* hands."

The intruder raised the knife high. This time, there was no glint. There was no indication the blade was there at all. Because it wasn't. It vanished from the intruder's grip as their hands plunged down toward the witch.

When the intruder's palm lay flat on her chest, the old witch sighed her last breath. She was gone.

Angry not to have killed her, not to have made her suffer, the intruder scoured the room for their prize, because the witch was wrong about one thing. They would find the book. And when they did, they'd set their plan into motion.

11

THE FACTION

The next morning, I rose before the sun, filled with dread for several reasons. It would be a long time before I got the image of Mr. Caulfield, dead as a doornail, out of my head.

And I still had to figure out what to do about magic and a familiar and vampires and werewolves.

And then there was that creepy podcast. I'd fallen asleep, but I listened to it again that morning. Creel Creek is strange. And getting stranger by the second.

I didn't think the hosts could be actual members of the paranormal community. No one is that stupid. *Are they?* But their voices did seem familiar...

Who could they be?

I shook my head. I didn't need to care. Gran manipulated me with magic to bring me here. I wanted to learn what I needed to learn and get out of here as fast as Crookshanks would go.

It still wasn't time to get up, but I was tired of being in bed. I needed to answer nature's calls. The first, to pee, and the second, much louder call for caffeine.

Today, I had nowhere to be. With the grocery closed indefinitely, I was probably out of a job. I doubted Mr. Caulfield had any relatives to take over the store in the event of his demise. Being a vampire, he probably assumed there wasn't going to be a demise.

I know that's how I'd play it.

On my first day, he'd given me a spiel about how the store had been passed down from generation to generation. I realized now that he must've actually passed it from himself to himself in some clever fashion—an old vampire trick, the way the Cullens maintained a residence in Forks for over a century. Oh, *Twilight*.

Again, my book knowledge proved much larger than my actual knowledge.

What would the residents of Creel Creek do without a grocery store? Surely, someone could buy it or take over. *But how long will that take? And will I still have a job when the dust settles?*

Definitely questions for another day.

I had more pressing matters to deal with—like when would my familiar show and who killed Mr. Caulfield.

More pressing even than that, I was finally ready to talk with Gran. Not about being a witch, not about a stupid dead vampire. I wanted to hear everything she could tell me about my mother.

I could forgive her trespasses if she'd just open up for once. I needed her. I wanted to know more about my mom.

Her snores were still reverberating throughout the house.

After I answered nature's call, I banged around in the kitchen, pretending to make coffee, until the racket was too much for her to take.

She shuffled into the kitchen in fuzzy slippers, her hair a

mess, her glasses crooked, and she looked like she needed a double dose of Nature's Miracle.

Stevie trailed in behind her. He too looked worse for wear with rumpled fur and droopy eyes.

Odd for a cat.

"Trouble sleeping?" I asked.

Gran took stock of the table. Two cups of coffee waited, steaming and ready to go.

"It's a trap," Stevie grumbled.

"And I thought you were cooking me breakfast. Banging pots and pans, slamming cabinets. And was that a tea whistle?"

"No, that was my lips."

"I should've known better."

"I told you," Stevie said. "Witches can't be trusted."

The cat had a solid argument.

Gran rounded on me. "This is about your mother, isn't it?"

I nodded. "But I still want to know why you look so—"

"Raggedy?" Stevie suggested. "Disheveled? Unkempt?"

"Unrested."

Gram scowled. "I was up late. I thought I'd ask the spirits if they knew anything about your dead vampire."

"He's not mine. He's ours. And did they?"

"When she says spirits," Stevie boomed, "she's mostly talking about booze."

"Rarely," Gran retorted. "Last night, I only had a sip."

This surprised me. Gran wasn't a drinker. And she hadn't been too interested in Mr. Caulfield's murder, other than me being a party to it—and she was right, it was totally her fault.

She dropped into her seat and drank half a cup of coffee before she came up for air.

"Well?" I asked.

"Well, what?"

"Did the spirits tell you anything?"

"No. They're as fickle as you were in high school. They didn't tell me anything we didn't already know, but they told me that old news twice or three times. Blood—they just kept saying the word blood. Over and over."

"He drank blood?"

"As vampires do," Gran said smartly. "Now, let me finish this coffee and we can discuss that other matter."

"My mother." Talking about Mr. Caulfield made it easy to forget what was really important to me. The lies I'd been told as a kid were hard to let go of. I still didn't know what to believe.

Gran made a show of slurping down the dregs.

Then she started.

"Your mother and I—our relationship was... trying. You know, I didn't always live in Creel Creek. Your mother grew up in—"

"Florida," I said.

"That's right. Her father, God rest his soul, was a good man. So young to die of a heart attack. But he came home early one day and walked in on me performing a spell. The shock killed him. Your mother blamed me. And magic.

"Your mother was raised by a single parent doing their best, just like you. Except my best doesn't measure up to the rest of 'em. Your mother left the day she turned eighteen, and I didn't see her again until the week before she turned forty."

Like me.

"I know what you're thinking. No, I didn't summon her. I realize now summoning you was a mistake. But, Constance, you can't come into your powers alone. Your mother knew that.

"By then, I'd moved here. I don't even know how she found me. You were with her, well, you probably don't remember. She made me enchant you to forget."

Correction. Apparently, I'd been to my Gran's house twice before.

"And she probably told your father she was on one of those location hunts."

"Thanks for telling me this," I told Gran. "I know it's hard."

"Oh, it's not so hard, owning up to my failures. The tricky thing is not repeating them. And that's where I'm afraid I've failed. Now, can I finish this story?"

"Go ahead," I encouraged her.

"It was like the past had never happened. We said our apologies and started fresh. You were an angel by the way. A lovely girl.

"But back to your mother. I couldn't believe it. Here, I thought for sure she'd renounce magic. But no. We had a birthday celebration. Your mother came into her powers. She bought every book Trish's mother had, from spells to curses, to potions and tonics. And she promised to keep in touch, which she did by calling me every week when she was really on a location hunt.

"My life had changed for the better. I couldn't believe it when she called to tell me about a job with the Faction." Gran gave me an expectant look.

Is that supposed to mean something to me?

"There's a faction?" I asked.

"Isn't there always?" Gran snorted. "A faction, an order... a ministry." That was a jab at me. Not to mention Arthur

Weasley, who works at the Ministry of Magic's Misuse of Muggle Artifacts office.

But that was something I hadn't considered. What type of jobs are there for witches?

"What kind of job was it?" I asked.

"She wouldn't say. She said it was a secret. That she'd call me again soon. And not to worry, you were in good hands with your father."

"I'm guessing this Faction doesn't advertise jobs on Glassed-In."

"Glassed what?"

I shook my head. "Never mind. It's an online job market and social network."

"Definitely not," Gran scoffed. "But they're not official in *our* world either. The Faction is one of those 'we'll police ourselves and tell everyone we're the good guys' kind of deals. And let's not even speculate where their money comes from."

"Well, *are* they the good guys?"

"In a manner of speaking."

Stevie, who'd been patiently grooming, snarled.

"I said, in a manner of speaking," Gran replied defensively. "That's the other thing. Familiars are an arcane tradition, and the Faction kills them on sight."

"They kill them? Really?"

I was stunned. This Faction didn't sound like anything out of my books. And they didn't sound like the good guys at all.

"Just their bodies." Gran sighed. "You can't actually kill—"

"No," Stevie interrupted, "you can do a lot worse. You can banish us to another plane of existence. One where we walk for eternity, alone."

"Oh, woe is me." Gran stroked his back. "Forced to live forever."

"So, my mother," I pressed, refusing to be distracted, "you think she... you think she joined this..."

My heart sank, but I didn't understand why. Not until a memory of a gray tabby cat popped into my head. My jaw dropped and I covered my mouth.

Gran knew. She wouldn't meet my eyes. "Stevie searched for your mother's familiar. But he was gone without a trace."

"Mr. Whiskers," I said, remembering the cat's name. "There's no way she killed him. She loved that cat. She loved her familiar. I remember."

"Mr. Whiskers," Stevie repeated. "He hated that name."

"And Serena always wanted him to be an owl."

"Mom would never have—"

"Nine out of ten times, isn't it the husband who kills the wife?" Stevie, still on edge, glared at me.

I didn't care. I knew there was no way my mother had betrayed Mr. Whiskers. There had to be another explanation why she'd join an order like this.

"So, that's it?" I asked. "That's the story? She joined this order—"

"Faction," Gran corrected.

I shook my head. "Okay. She joined *the Faction* and was never heard from again."

"That about sums it up," Gran said.

I preferred the plane crash. At least it had given me closure.

Gran got up and made eggs. While she hadn't given me much more, it was enough to solidify my decision about Creel Creek. Not only was I going to stay and come into my magic, I was going to find out everything I could about the Faction.

12

IN WITCH I MEET MY FAMILIAR

The rest of the day crawled by. I spent it with Gran. First up, *The Price Is Right*, then reruns of Jessica Fletcher, and by late afternoon when *Judge Judy* slammed down her gavel, it was a relief. Gran watched her nighttime dramas while I cooked dinner.

There was no way I could take this for two days in a row. So, when I woke the next morning, I resolved to accomplish something.

With no word from Trish or anyone about the grocery, I assumed my usual morning shift was canceled. Nothing about the murder on the news or the paper's Facebook page. Disappointed the killer was still on the loose, I pondered what I should do with my morning. I wasn't going to wake up Gran two days in a row, so I opted to get out of the house —and also get out of my head.

I know most runners use their morning jogs for introspection. Not me—the act of running taxes my mental facilities as much as it does my knees and hip joints. I have to concentrate on breathing while my heart screams at the exertion.

Quickly, I changed into a pair of shorts, an old tank top, and an even older pair of sneakers. I stretched, then limbered up with a few drills. I looped through the subdivision on my way to the clay road running between the neighborhood and the cemetery.

The road circled the cemetery and met the highway. I continued down the shoulder, picking up the pace as the road straightened coming into town. I was constantly using mental tricks on myself, lying, telling my body I would stop at the next intersection or that I'd turn around when I'd gone a mile.

I made it all the way to the Creel Creek Welcomes You sign before I had to stop and come up for air.

I laced my fingers together and put them behind my head like track stars do after a hard run. It didn't help. I fought the urge to hunch like Quasimodo and suck wind.

Lactic acid had already built up in my quads.

There was no way I had enough energy in the tank to trudge home. This was why running and I didn't get along. It's not therapeutic, not in the way Runner's World makes it out to be. It's more like a deep tissue massage from one of those chairs at the mall.

And it got worse. The famous fog rolled in with the rising sun and was knee deep already. While I was internally complaining about the fog, I noticed something strange.

A little side road leading to a park, and on the other side of the park, a library.

I'd driven past that spot dozens of times, and all I'd ever seen was a hill and some trees. Well, it was still a hill and some trees, but now they were enclosed by a wrought iron fence with a gate that teetered on the border between ornate and sinister. The frightening if over-embellished gate opened to a path much too gravelly for running. Under the trees, I spied a rusty swing set, though the chains and the seats dangling from it looked new.

I took the path at moderate pace, hoping to prevent my legs from getting stiff.

Something rustled under a nearby tree, startling me. I laughed at myself when I realized it was just a squirrel.

Why does that squirrel look so judgy? Then the penny dropped. *A familiar... my familiar. It has to be.*

After all, I was finally clear about this whole witch thing. I'd come not only to accept it, but to appreciate the possibilities. I was going to find out about my mother—what really happened to her.

"Hello, little guy."

He straightened, the way squirrels do before deciding whether to bolt all the way across a road when a car is coming or if they should stop in front of it. He bolted, zigzagging across the path and up a tree.

"Talking to strange animals?" The voice came from all around me, low and resonant, like Stevie's. "You must have bigger problems than I thought. And *those* were bad—a dead vampire, your only friend is a witch you don't trust who reveres your grandmother—who also happens to be a witch you don't trust."

I whipped around, searching for the voice's owner. There were no squirrels, no cats. I scanned the trees for that owl I kept hearing. But the branches were empty.

Then a set of ears emerged from behind a stump ringed with oyster mushrooms. I craned my neck to get a better look at what surely was my familiar.

Another woodland creature—not a squirrel—regarded me.

A raccoon. It climbed onto the stump, pulling itself with

paws that looked very much like hands. It sat down, crossing one foot over the other like a human woman sitting down in a chair.

"You've been watching me this whole time," I accused.

"Define whole time."

"For several days."

"Oh. Then, yes."

"And I wasn't talking to the squirrel," I said. "I saw it there and thought it must be... I thought it must be you."

"Me?" the raccoon scoffed. "That repugnant little thing? Heavens, no."

The squirrel chittered at us from a branch overhead.

The raccoon trilled and shook his fist. The squirrel decided retreat was in order and disappeared.

"You know," he said, "you never so much as looked in my direction when I was watching you, so I thought I'd better introduce myself."

"Okay, introduce yourself. I'm Constance, but you already knew that."

"And my name is unpronounceable by a human voice. So, you got one for me, or do we need to choose?"

"I, uh, I didn't know I'd have to name you."

"Honestly, it's not rocket science," my familiar boomed. "That is an expression that you humans still use, right?"

"It is," I said. But I knew his name now.

I have an affinity for Rocket Raccoon from Marvel's *Guardians of the Galaxy*. But Rocket was too on the nose.

"Brad," I said, envisioning the gorgeous actor who voices him. "You're Brad."

"Brad." My familiar smiled the way all pets do when they're happy or dehydrated. "I like it. I like it a lot. This body though, it's a bit different. I can't believe you thought I'd be a—"

"You're really going to criticize squirrels? *You?*" I said.

"Why? He looked down. "Wait—what is it? What am I?"

"You really don't know?"

"I'm not that up on Earthly species. And honestly, I thought this was what you wanted me to be."

"What I wanted?" I was flabbergasted.

Why on Earth would my familiar think I wanted a trash panda?

"How would you know what I wanted?"

"The other—the cat you talked to last night—it told you we can read minds, correct?"

"He did. But—but I never pictured you as a raccoon. I only—"

"You pictured things you didn't want me to be. I had to do some digging. Deep in the recesses of your mind, I found this, and I thought—"

"You went digging?" I was appalled. "But Stevie said you could only see what I was thinking."

"No, Stevie—I'm guessing that's your grandmother's familiar—said *vampires* could only see what you were thinking. You assumed the same was true of familiars, but they never said any such thing. This Stevie, I think I knew him by a different name upstairs."

"You knew him?"

"It was a long time ago in a realm far, far away. I thought they were fools for coming to Earth. Now look at me, I'm on Earth and I'm a... trash panda? Is that what you called it?"

"Raccoon," I corrected.

"No, I'm pretty sure you thought trash panda."

He was right, I had thought it.

But Brad was adorable, though all raccoons are cute when they're not knocking over trash cans. A little plump around the middle, his eyes were beady and black and inside the mask. His whiskers were long and catlike.

"Wait," I said. "Do you mean this is your first time on Earth? And your first time as a familiar?" I shouldn't've sounded so horrified, but that's how it came out.

I'd probably offended him. To think, this was the being I was meant to spend the rest of my life with.

"Correct." The raccoon scratched its chin thoughtfully, more human than animal.

In the few days I'd known about Stevie, the only human-like trait he'd shown was talking. Otherwise, he seemed like an ordinary cat. He used a litter box, for heaven's sake.

"Wait, Stevie said that familiars were fallen angels—neutrals in heaven's war."

"Did he not explain that the war between heaven and hell rages even today?"

I shook my head.

"If things were all hunky-dory up there, do you think things down here would be what they are? God left this place to its own devices eons ago. I thought that much was obvious."

"Well, when you say it like that," I said. "But why now? I mean, why'd you leave?"

"I was tired of being a soldier. Tired of being used."

"And this is better?" I wasn't so sure. "You're trapped in the body of a raccoon."

"Well, I didn't know I'd be a raccoon, now did I?" Brad snarled. "I'm sure the next girl will have better taste in movies."

"It's not entirely my fault," I protested. "I didn't ask for you to be a raccoon. I was kind of hoping for a dog. But you went digging without an invitation and wandered into my memories of *Guardians of the Galaxy*."

"Guardians of what?"

"The galaxy." I sighed. "Don't worry about it. It's a movie. Have you heard of movies?"

"We're familiar with your culture, yes." He leaped down from the stump. "Now, let's get home. I'm starving. Names, shelter, food—all your department, my dear witch," he announced. "Remember, to the outside world I have to look like a pet."

"To the outside world you're a nuisance," I said. "I can't exactly take you to Home Depot. Are you sure you can't change into a dog?"

"As much as I'd like to, no. This is my form."

"Shame."

I got on my feet and discovered my legs were stiff and sore. There was no way I was going to be running home. It was going to be a long walk. The raccoon followed.

"Don't do that," I said.

"Don't do what?"

"Walk on your hind legs," I scolded. "It's creepy. Raccoons don't walk like that for very long."

"Understood." He trotted awkwardly, front paws, then back. "Anything else I should know?"

"Yes," I said, stopping abruptly. "Humans don't usually associate with raccoons. So being seen with you right now is probably not such a good thing."

And there were definitely humans headed our way.

A pearl-white minivan eased into the gravel parking lot, tires crunching, and rolled to a stop.

Brad was gone. When I saw who was getting out of the van, part of me wished I could disappear, too.

13

IN WITCH I MEET THE FAMILY

Three young girls emerged from the van and raced for the swing set.

"I want the good swing," the smallest of the three yelled.

"No, I get it," the middle girl proclaimed. "Dad said I could, in the car!"

"I said no such thing."

Sheriff Dave Marsters still had his mustache and his smile. But he wasn't wearing his ball cap or uniform. He nodded in my direction.

The girls swooshed by me, sprinting down the path without giving me so much as a look. The tallest, and probably oldest, of the girls was first to the swings. She hopped on what I assumed to be the "good swing."

"No fair!" the youngest pouted. "You *always* get it."

"Not always." The middle girl took another swing. This one was higher off the ground than the other, probably too tall for the smallest girl anyway.

"You only get it when I let you win," the older girl said.

They both shuffled back and let go at almost the same time, beginning to pump. The littlest waited on Dad.

But Dave stopped at the gate holding two frisbees and a soccer ball and gave me a once over. I more than probably looked a mess, sweaty and in my ratty running attire.

"You went for a run this morning?"

"Is it that obvious?" I joked. "I just found this place."

"I'm impressed. This is quite a ways from your grandma's place, isn't it?"

"That it is," I said. "I was actually about to head back now."

"Oh, don't *run* off on our account," he said cheerfully. "They're friendly when they aren't so preoccupied. One-track minds—it's all about the *good* swing. And I see Allie got it."

"Allie," I repeated.

He nodded. "Elsie's in the middle, and the little one is Kacie. And yes, there's a bit of a theme with the naming. You can meet them, if you like. Kacie's going to be mad if I don't get there soon."

"Don't let me stop you."

"No, no. I do all the *stopping* around these parts." He winked.

I should've been offended, but it was a good joke.

I did a quick scan for Brad, didn't see him, and gave the girls on the swings one last look. They were cuties. But he was right, the little one, Allie, had her arms crossed. She was ready for a push from Dad.

"I've got to get going," I said. "I've already let my legs stiffen up enough. As it is, the next couple of miles are going to be a challenge. And I don't want to intrude."

"Next couple of miles?" He scrunched his face. His

mustache twisted into the shape of an M. "Your grandma's place has to be five miles from here."

Five miles? It had felt like a long way, but not that long. If I ran back I'd be doing close to a half marathon today, something I'd only done once, when I turned thirty. And that was after months and months of training.

"Come on. It won't be an intrusion," he reassured me. "And I'd be happy to drop you off. Actually, I need to pay a visit to your grandmother anyway—in a more professional capacity."

"About the..."

"About the murder, yeah."

Dave had been inching down the path, and without really noticing it, I'd kept up. We were almost two-thirds of the way to the swings.

"Come on," he said again. "Meet the girls. Just don't talk about the M-U-R-D-E-R."

"I know how to spell, Dad," the oldest girl, Allie, said.

"I do too!" Elsie whispered to her sister. "What did he spell?"

"Murder," Allie whispered back.

"What's murder?"

"Push me." Kacie flailed her arms in her father's direction. "Daddy, you took too long."

"I'm sorry," the sheriff soothed. "Girls, I want y'all to meet my friend, Constance. She works at the grocery."

"Where there was a murder," Allie blurted.

"What's a murder?" Elsie asked.

"It's—it's nothing y'all need to worry about. Police business. What do we say about police business?"

"It's for you to know, and us not to," Kacie recited promptly.

Dave joined his daughter at the swings, and soon, she was flying as high as her sisters.

"That's right. It's for me to know."

"But you tell us about Mr. Palicki all the time," Elsie countered.

Her dad just shook his head. "That's because Mr. Palicki doesn't hurt anyone but himself." To me, he said, "Town drunk. We took his driver's license away years ago, but I can't get it through his head that bicycling while intoxicated is *also* a crime."

"You said he needs training wheels like me," Elsie giggled. "Except I don't need them anymore. You're just being over... overprotective."

"No," Dave sighed. "I just haven't had the time to take them off. I will. I promise."

"Miss," Elsie said, "will you push me?"

"Her name is Constance. And she doesn't have to push you. You're six years old and you can do it yourself."

"But I can't go as high as Allie," she protested. "Not without a boost."

"Do you mind?" Dave asked, unsure.

I remembered Trish saying he hadn't dated since his wife passed. These three were the reasons why. They were good reasons.

I smiled. "I'll push you—as long as you don't mind going over the bar!"

"No way!" Elsie exclaimed. "Allie says she saw someone go over the bar, and it made his skin come off."

"That's not true."

"What's not true?" Dave asked. "That you *said* it or that his skin came off?"

"It was just a fib, Daddy. Elsie shouldn't be so gullible."

"What does gullible mean?" Elsie asked.

"You're not supposed to fib!" Kacie proclaimed, smugly content since her dad started pushing her.

"That's true," the sheriff agreed. "But we all do from time to time. I'm pretty sure I heard a few tall tales the other day."

"Not from me." My heart raced. Did the sheriff think I was lying about Mr. Caulfield?

"No, no. Not from you. And probably not about the M-U-R-D-E-R either."

"We know that spells murder, Dad," Elsie said scornfully. She just didn't know what it meant.

He grinned, then shrugged. "We'll talk about it later—without these acute ears."

"My ears aren't cute," Kacie grumbled. "He won't let get me earrings."

"I have earrings." Elsie shook the blonde curls around her ears to show me. "So does Allie. Our mom took us."

Her father's face fell. "I'm just not ready yet. Mom did that kind of thing. And I can't stand to see you girls cry."

"It doesn't hurt." Allie was the first off her swing—the good one. She jumped at the high end of the arc and landed gracefully on her feet.

Elsie did the same, less gracefully. "Yeah, Dad, it doesn't hurt."

"Y'all just don't remember. Trust me. It hurts. I got one when I was seventeen." He pointed to his left ear, which was currently earringless. There was the slightest of indentions where the hole had been.

"Did you cry, Daddy?" Kacie asked.

"No, but I wanted to."

Dave dropped the soccer ball and kicked it Allie's way. The girls went off to a grassy spot beneath the trees, close to where I'd found Brad.

I wondered where he'd gotten off to. I scanned the trees again and saw a few more squirrels but no raccoon.

"Do you mind pushing Kacie for a few minutes?" the sheriff asked. "I'm going to kick the ball around, then we'll take you home."

"Sure." Pushing Kacie was a lot easier than pushing her older sister.

"Are you going to the carnival?" she asked when she was moving again.

"What carnival?"

"The summer carnival, silly. It's fun. We eat candy and stay up all night."

"She means the Midsummer Festival," Dave called. "It's in a couple weeks."

"Oh. I don't know," I told her.

"Okay." She shrugged, already over it.

After about ten minutes, she was ready to join her sisters. They included both of us in their little soccer match, but we were out of our element. And my legs weren't having it.

The sun was burning through the morning layer of fog. It was hot, and my shirt was sticky with sweat. We all climbed in the van, and they drove me to Gran's house. I didn't see a raccoon anywhere.

The second their van was out of sight, his bandit face appeared over the edge of the front porch, and he climbed up after it.

I opened the door, and he barged in ahead of me. "I'm home," Brad boomed for the whole house to hear.

14

DAYLIGHT

My familiar made it to the kitchen where he was greeted by a yelp from Gran. She was expecting a cat. Gran seemed about as ready to see Brad as I'd been to hear Stevie talk.

"You weren't kidding about the trash panda thing," Brad said to me.

Recovered from her momentary fright, Gran pursed her lips and said, "This *should* go without saying, but just in case, you *won't* be digging through my garbage."

"I won't," he agreed. "But I am starving. It was a struggle last night. These bodies come with a whole host of quirks. Luckily, I found the cat food your neighbor leaves out. Then *someone* chased me away."

Stevie strolled into the kitchen and looked the raccoon over, pleased not to see a rat or bird. "That was you? I thought you were a real raccoon, hanging around in my territory."

Brad said something unintelligible.

Stevie replied, a greeting of sorts. Not in our language—not in any language spoken on Earth. Indecipherable, it had the grinding discord of metal on metal. Some of it sounded like Latin. Some had the fluidity of French, and some had the twang of most Asian dialects. But on the whole, it sounded like a NASCAR race in Gran's kitchen.

"That's about enough of that nonsense," Gran said sternly, waving her caution flag.

She really was a nice old woman. She didn't look like anything fierce. It was only in the last few days my perspective had changed. I could sense the power behind those pale blue eyes.

"When you're in my house," she lectured, "you'll speak *our* language. And who, may I ask, are you?"

"He's my familiar," I said.

"Hon, I know that. I was asking for a name."

The raccoon answered with more metal on metal sound.

"I meant your *other* name," Gran said. "I'll never be able to pronounce that one."

"His name's Brad," I offered, but no one was paying any attention to me.

Stevie was focused on the raccoon. He repeated the unpronounceable name, saying, "When we were both upstairs, I never thought you'd be one to defect."

Brad shrugged, his paws palm side up. "We all change—humans and celestial beings alike. And as for my Earthly name, I think we decided on Brad—right before that wolf and his cubs showed up."

"Wolf?" Gran asked. "What wolf? Constance, where have you been all morning?"

I looked at my sweaty clothes pointedly, as if sweaty in ratty clothes would mean anything to Gran.

"I went for a run," I said. "You know there's a park at the edge of town? That's where I met Brad. And Sheriff Marsters was there with his daughters."

"That's nice," Gran said.

"He dropped me off. He said he's going to come by later —in, uh, more *professional* capacity."

"When?" Gran flushed.

I shrugged.

"This house is a mess. Did he happen to say if it'd be lunch time? I could cook him something. I don't know if he likes—"

"Gran," I interrupted, to slow her down, "he didn't say. And I doubt he wants a Stouffer's. Here, I'll help you clean up a bit."

I'd never seen her get spun up so fast. The way she lived I'd never have imagined she cared what the house looked like to anyone else.

"I'll have to do my hair," she said. "And I'd hate if he saw me without my face on. I only hope I can help with the case."

So far, she'd ignored the fact it was a professional visit from the police, getting flustered over trivialities like her face instead. Sure, he was cute. And seeing the way he interacted with his girls was charming. But Gran was more than twice his age. If anyone needed to put on a face, it was me.

Then I wondered how she thought she was going to help.

"I thought you said the spirits were useless."

"Yes, yes." She shook her head at me like I was stupid. "But there are other ways I can help—just like I did when that Miller boy went missing three years ago. It was horrible, but that's a story for another time."

"How horrible?" My brain didn't trust I'd remember to ask her. After all, it had taken me a day to follow up about Mom.

"Oh, we found him, if that's what you're worried about.

He was fine and dandy. And he still is as far as I know. It was everything else that was horrible. Now, let's see about this mess."

Gran clasped her hands together at her chest and chanted,

"Spick and span, dust every fan,
tend to the clutter and rot.
Make this house gleam when I say clean,
now, clean and don't miss a spot."

I EXPECTED *FANTASIA*. I expected the brooms and the mops to go to work and get unruly—because don't they always get unruly?

I was disappointed.

The dust and grime vanished as if it'd never been there. Over the past few weeks, I'd mopped and scrubbed and put away. I'd spent hours toiling on the mess when it was no trouble for Gran's magic at all.

What the heck?

"Now, hair," she said.

I waited for her to cast another spell, but she headed for the bathroom. I followed.

The cat and the raccoon disappeared, either to be out of the way for the sheriff's visit, or more likely, to get reacquainted.

"Well," I said when we reached the bathroom, "what do you do for hair? I might need to know when I get my powers."

"Oh, there's no spell for hair, my girl. Just a whole lot of hairspray."

GRAN DID her hair and put on her face—which meant some blush and a touch of lipstick.

I showered and did the same.

The sheriff showed up in the early afternoon in the police SUV, wearing his uniform.

I managed to talk Gran out of making him lunch. She baked cookies instead. I made tea.

"I'm actually watching my weight," he told us regretfully. "Or I've *been* watching it... go up and up. If you can pack them to go, the girls would devour some homemade cookies."

I smiled at his lame joke and the thought of his daughters. I could only imagine what it was like to raise three. My dad had his hands full with just the one.

"I'm sure I have some Tupperware here somewhere," Gran said.

I knew the closest thing in her cabinets were old Cool Whip containers.

"Here we go." It took some whispered words and a whirl of her finger, but she produced Tupperware.

"And you'll have tea, won't you, Sheriff?" she asked him.

"Tea's fine," he agreed. "And it's Dave. Both of you, please call me Dave."

We all took a seat at the kitchen table. I couldn't help but be reminded of Gran and Stevie breaking the news to me. Just a couple of days later and I was sitting here beside a werewolf. Not that there was currently anything wolfish about him aside from the stubble on his cheeks.

Are all werewolves so hairy?

"So," Gran said, "how can we help you?"

"Daylight," Dave replied. "I don't know much about it—just some things my mom told me. And what I heard on the street growing up. But I doubt much of that's true."

Gran bobbed her head knowingly.

"I've been wondering about it too," I said. "I saw Mr. Caulfield in the daytime. Was he—I mean are vampires *really* vulnerable to the sun?"

"Not the sun," Gran explained. "Daylight is a drug of sorts—a potion, *usually* brewed by a witch."

"That much, I knew," Dave acknowledged.

"What kind of potion? What does it do?"

"Well," Gran said, "it's a drug for werewolves. It counters the effects of moonlight, so they don't change into a wolf during the full moon. Hence the name, daylight."

"That sounds convenient."

"It is, but it's not," Dave cut in. "From what I understand—what I was warned about in my youth—is that there are some bad side effects. My mom never said much more."

"Your mom, she was a—"

He nodded. "A werewolf, yes. So was Dad, but he didn't like to talk about it much. He was one of those who believe it's a curse. He blamed witches. And he hated vampires. Not really a nice man, my dad."

"Understatement of the century," Gran chortled. "But he was right to give *some* witches a wide berth."

"Okay, what are the side effects?" I wanted to move things along. It felt like all I'd gotten was history lessons—lectures, when I wanted answers to the quiz.

Gran scowled at me. "They still need to turn into the wolf. You see, it's not really the moon that causes the transformation, it's the cycle. And missing a cycle, well, you're a woman, I'm sure you can understand."

The sheriff didn't want to touch that remark.

"And daylight," he said, "it's addictive. I heard of someone who took the stuff for years, then when they went off it—they ran out—they were in wolf form for months, terrorizing the town they lived in. There's no coming back from that."

"Then why take it?" I asked. I wasn't getting the full picture. What was the point of this drug?

"You know how during the witch trials women got dunked under water?" Dave asked. "If they sank, and drowned, they were innocent. If they floated, they were a witch."

"Totally irrelevant by the way," Gran said. "Everyone sinks—witches and men and women alike."

"Right. Werewolves too," Dave agreed. "Anyway, the same kind of thing happens to werewolves every now and again. We have to *prove* our innocence by staying human during the full moon."

"Which proved difficult."

"It did," Gran agreed. "So, a friendly neighborhood witch decided to help. She concocted the daylight potion."

"So friendly." I listed the side effects in my head. It was like one of those pharmaceutical commercials. The last thirty seconds is devoted to the harmful things the drug can do.

"Hey—it's not our fault," Gran retorted. "That's nature for you."

"And it's lethal to vampires?"

"It seems so," Dave said. "The, uh, forensic folks found a trace of something in Mr. Caulfield's morning coffee. And not just blood—because there was some of that too."

Gran's mind was moving faster than mine. "Given what Trish found—the word daylight—you suspect that's what it was?"

"That's right."

"And you came here to ask me to brew you some." It wasn't a question. Gran knew why Dave was here. "You want me to brew it, so you can make sure you're correct."

He sighed. "That's right. I just need it to compare with the evidence we have. I mean, if it's possible for you to—"

"Oh, it's possible," Gran told him. "It will take about a week."

Dave thanked us for our time, and Gran for brewing the potion.

I walked him to the door, my head still spinning over daylight and vampires. The way it just clicked. The way it made sense—almost the opposite of hearing the story about my mother.

"What about other myths?" I asked. "Silver bullets? Stakes to the heart?"

"I don't care what it is." Dave grinned. "It's going to die when you put a stake through its heart. As for silver bullets, well, I'm hoping to never find out."

15

IN WITCH I GO TO THE TOP OF THE HILL

A raccoon was curled against my hip. Like a dog, he opened one eye when I stirred but without really waking. I left him in bed and went down to the kitchen for much-needed coffee.

The kitchen tables had turned. This time, Gran was there waiting for me with a cup already in hand.

"Tonight's the big night," she said with glee. She took a sip and steam fogged her glasses, making her ratty old pink robe and bunny slippers look even more ridiculous. Her bedhead was dire—party on the left side, flattened on the right.

"Tonight? What's tonight?"

"The ritual," she said. "Your coming of age."

As if I needed the reminder. My joints were stiff and my back ached from letting a varmint sleep against it.

"Party. Ritual. Same thing."

"Except my birthday is tomorrow."

"The funny thing about birthdays," Gran said, "is they start at midnight and they last all day."

Obviously, that was true. But did she really expect me, or anyone else for that matter, to stay out so late?

"Okay. I'm beginning to understand this place is some sort of hotbed for paranormal activity. Full of witches, werewolves, and vampires—"

"It was just the one vampire actually," Gran corrected.

"Right. I get it. I do. There's you and there's Trish but, uh, who else is invited to this thing?"

Gran counted off the names on her fingers. "Well, you know Trish. And you know our neighbor down the way, Agatha."

"This is the first I've heard about her being a witch," I said. I took my seat across from Gran.

"She's really good with simple spells, that one. Not a potion maker—hence the reason your crush came a knockin' on my door."

"He's not my—"

Gran eyed me in a way that said don't argue.

"Okay, he's interesting," I admitted. "But I'm not a fan of that mustache. Those girls though... they were so cute."

"Moving on..." Gran smirked. "There's Hilda Jeffries. She lives across town. I'm not a huge fan of Kalene Moone—I might've accidentally forgotten to send out her invitation. Although, I'm hoping Lauren Whittaker shows. Lord help us if Nell Baker does. She's as stereotypical a witch as they come."

That was interesting. "What do you mean?"

"Well, I don't think she's ever boiled any children. But let's just say I wouldn't be too surprised if her house was made of gingerbread or if she had a flying monkey or two."

I tried to picture such a woman, though I highly doubted my imagination lined up with the real thing. For one, most people don't have green skin.

Gran said, "All the local witches are invited. That doesn't mean they'll all show. We usually get half as many as I'd like, and of the ones we do get, I like less than half."

"Should we cook something?" I asked. Luckily, Gran had taken care of cleaning with a wiggle of her finger the day before.

"Oh, no." Gran shook her head. "We'll be meeting them in the graveyard. Our magic is ten times more powerful in the witching hour—and almost fifty times more potent if done on hallowed ground."

"Really?" I wasn't asking about the magic. I wanted to know if my fortieth birthday party was going to be in a graveyard.

"It's more complicated than that," Gran explained. "A full moon, a blood moon, a solstice—any pagan holiday—will have an effect on the amount of magic in the air. There are some spells, mostly curses, that can only be done inside the witching hour. That's from the stroke of midnight to one in the morning."

"And things like cleaning can be done whenever." I whirled my finger the way Gran had.

"Yes," Gran agreed. "But had I done it at midnight, we'd be looking at a whole new house. Spick and span."

"And that's why Trish's summoning charm only produced the one word."

"Summoning is extra tricky. You can't just do it for fun. You have to have a great need. For example, I can't just will that spatula to me when I'm perfectly capable of walking over there and getting it."

"That doesn't make any sense. Yesterday, you were capable of cleaning a whole house."

"No," Gran disagreed. "I didn't have the time to do it. I had the need and no time. Trust me. I tried it before you got here, and nothing happened. The magic must not've thought you needed to see a clean house."

"But good ol' Dave did?" I asked.

Gran huffed.

I was beginning to understand that magic was something I'd never truly comprehend. Like people, it was fickle. But it was also smart. I couldn't tell Gran how much the magic was right. Had I walked into a clean house instead of finding the place in disarray, I might very well have walked right back out.

Instead of creeping around a graveyard tonight, I thought, *I'd be in California having a pre-birthday dinner with my dad.*

We Skyped later that day, since he was going to be busy on my actual birthday. He also claimed there was a card in the mail, which I knew meant that he'd get around to sending one in the next day or two.

Dad hadn't been very happy to hear about my boss's untimely demise. He even threatened to retrieve me from Virginia.

I think Gran put a stop to that—there was possibly some magic involved. I could've sworn I saw her twirl her finger under the table and whisper something. Dad calmed down and we ended the call.

"Do you always twirl your finger like that?" I asked, firmly closing the laptop.

"Not always."

"Always," Stevie boomed. "It's kind of her thing."

"It's not my thing."

The cat winked at me.

Brad chose this moment to show himself. He scooted backward down the stairs on unsure feet.

"It takes a while to get used to stairs," Stevie told him.

"I have to get used to a lot of things." Brad studied his

paws and shuddered. "I wasn't expecting this transition to be so difficult."

"It would've been worse if you were a rodent," Gran said. Then to Stevie, "And I don't *always* twirl my finger."

"You never answered me," I cut in. "When you told me I was a witch, I asked about a wand. I wanted to see yours. I guess that's it, huh?"

"Would you prefer I go pull a stick from the tree outside? Or better yet, I'll make you one from unicorn hair. Let me just find a unicorn."

"Okay. Okay." I smiled. "No wands. No unicorns. I just hoped *something* was like the movies."

"Why would we use wands if we don't have to?" Gran asked. "Seems rather inconvenient, if I'm being honest. Oh wait, sorry, I forgot my wand at home. Left it in the lockbox with my pistol."

"Gran!"

"What?" She laughed. "That's what those movies make them out to be, don't they? Weapons. They can't go anywhere without a magic revolver in their pocket. See—" She pointed her finger at me. "I'm always packing heat."

Then she pointed to the last of the morning's coffee, now barely lukewarm. The glass glowed bright orange and steam billowed from it.

"You didn't say a rhyme," I observed. "And you could've used the microwave. See—magic makes no sense."

"A good phrase will do in a pinch," Gran said. "And the pot *isn't* microwave safe."

"Your cup is though," I pointed out as she filled it.

We spent the rest of the day watching made-for-TV movies and taking turns catnapping with her cats and the familiars. Brad's raccoon inclinations made it tough for him to be awake for the better part of the day.

I made dinner and was ready for real sleep when Gran started shuffling from room to room as if she was looking for her keys. But I could hear her keys jingling. And she never drove her car if she could get out of it.

"It's time. It's time." She scooted past where I was curled up on the couch and scoured the TV stand for whatever it was she'd lost. "Now, where did I put it?"

"Where did you put what?"

"My ring," Gran said. "It's the only way to see into the darkness."

"You've never heard of a flashlight?"

"You don't need a ring when you have us," Brad said. He and Stevie were waiting at the door like dogs waiting to be let out.

"While that's true most of the time, it isn't true in the graveyard."

"We aren't allowed inside," Stevie told Brad. "Witches rules."

"What good are we if we aren't able to perform our duties?" Brad asked.

Cats can't shrug, but somehow Stevie managed it.

"What are they on about?" I asked Gran.

Gran ignored me. She let out a shriek, digging through an old box of even older TV Guides. "Found it!"

A ruby red ring glimmered in the dim light from the kitchen. Gran took up a post beside the familiars at the door. "Well, are you coming?"

"It's only 11:00," I objected. "The cemetery is like two minutes away."

Gran shook her head.

There's always a catch. I waited for it to come out of Gran's mouth.

"The cemetery, yes. But I said graveyard. They aren't one and the same."

Before I could get a word in, the old broad was out the door, familiars trotting after her. And instead of heading to my car, Gran veered toward the woods behind the house. I had to hurry to catch up.

"Nothing like a midnight stroll through bear-infested woods," I said sarcastically.

"Bears here aren't nocturnal," Gran hissed. "Didn't you learn anything in school? And I wouldn't call it infested. Not exactly."

"It's a loose quote from one of my favorite movies."

"A Harry Potter?"

"*The Princess Bride*."

"I'm not a fan of princesses."

Gran studied the ground ahead of us and turned down a faint path. "And if anything," she said, "I'd be worried about the coyotes."

The barely-there trail twisted into the wood. Brad and Stevie stayed beside us, their silhouettes flickering in the moonlight. Sometimes animal, sometimes not.

We came to a clearing around a sloping hill. I could just make out the graveyard on the other side. Unlike the cemetery with its chain-link fence, this graveyard had wrought iron. And its gate was much like the gate to the park I'd discovered, only much more ominous.

A crescent moon, brighter than any sliver of moon had the right to be, lit up the clearing.

This was exactly the type of place people had nightmares about—dreams of spooky graveyards where demons, vampires, and witches lurked. It was the type of place that gave me chills. It felt like we shouldn't be here.

I said as much to Gran.

"Witches are the only people with the right to be in a graveyard at midnight," she said. "It's the only time the spirits truly sleep."

"You don't mean—"

"That's exactly what I mean."

I don't know what I'd thought she meant when she talked about speaking to spirits. A Ouija Board came to mind, not actual spirits. I added ghosts to the ever-growing queue of mythical creatures I didn't believe existed until moving to Creel Creek, Virginia.

The familiars had stopped ahead of the gate. I turned back. Something about them looked off. Translucent. If I tried to pet Brad, I thought my arm would go right through him.

"Come on." Gran held up her hand and pushed, and the gates flew open. "They're waiting on us."

Waiting for us up on the hill were five more women.

"You know Trish and Agatha," Gran said. "This here is Hilda Jefferies."

Hilda was the tallest of the bunch. Taller by a head than the others, close to my height with a dark complexion.

"And Lauren Whittaker, she lives in Charlottesville but tries to make it over when she can. We're so glad to have you." Lauren, who could only be a year or so older than me, shook my hand. She had chin-length dark hair and big blue eyes.

"And Kalene," Gran said with an edge to her voice. "I'm so glad you made it."

A short mound of a woman gave Gran a curt smile. Kalene was pushing past forty into fifty. She had dark curls the size of fists down to her elbows.

"I just heard from Lauren," Kalene said, "that we're adding another to our coven."

Gran, barely fazed by Kalene's gate-crashing, smiled. "I've told you time and again, we *aren't* a coven. We're five, now six, witches who meet on occasion to trade curses and spells. We're together in solidarity but singular in magic."

"You two aren't singular," Kalene pointed out.

"Constance, under my tutelage, will maintain the lineage of my family. She'll obey the rules and the tenets of our order."

"*As witches we toil. As witches we make*," the witches chanted together with Kalene just slightly off beat.

"I just think it'd be better if we were a *real* coven," Kalene added. "If we shared our magic equally, not playing favorites." She eyed me, then Trish.

"You think this is all because your mother left us ten years ago, don't you?" Hilda stooped down and wrapped an arm around Kalene's shoulder. "Trust me, dear. We were just as disorganized when your mother was here."

Lauren shrugged at me. "It was before my time too."

"Mine too," Trish said.

Despite the fact that this meeting was supposed to be about me coming into my witch-hood, I realized there were other things in play. There was history here, history that I couldn't learn in one night. Something I couldn't learn in weeks. It would take time to get to know these women.

I wasn't going to let Gran's cynicism cloud my judgment. I hoped to get to know Kalene and Lauren just as I had Trish. If I stayed in Creel Creek, the three of us would be the future of whatever this group would become, be it a coven or single witches together in solidarity.

Gran *hmphed*. Then she nodded to us and started up the hill toward the lone tree standing atop it. We followed.

She reached the tree and put her palm against it. The

others did the same in turn. I put my hand on the coarse bark last.

"Let's do what we came here to do," Gran said. "Each witch will bestow a gift on you, Constance. A gift to last a year and a day, running out at the stroke of midnight that ends your next birthday. These enchantments will ease the transition from the world you knew. May they comfort or protect or aid you."

Gran turned to the other witches. "And remember, only grant what you have to spare—what you can stand to live without for a year."

"Who goes first?" Agatha asked.

"You're as good as any," Gran told her.

Agatha closed her eyes as if meditating. Her hand went rigid, then it glowed as Gran's had done when she warmed the coffee.

Immediately, I felt the heat of it. It took all of my willpower not to draw away in surprise. Yet somehow, my body sensed this warmth was mine to have, and I relaxed into it like a hot bath.

"I grant you enhanced comprehension of spell books."

Hilda went next. "I grant you protection from potions aiming to do you harm."

"Hilda," Gran scolded, "we talked about this. Didn't you learn anything from Trish?"

I let the magic flow through me before I asked, "What's wrong?"

Trish leaned in. "While it sounds good in theory, it also nullifies the effects of alcohol."

"Oh, that's too bad."

Trish muttered under her breath, "Worst year of my life."

"You next," Gran told her.

Trish had to think a moment. She squinted at the moon then decided. "I grant you protection from Halitosis Hal. May all of his advances be thwarted."

"You're giving that up?" I asked her.

"It's not a big deal for me. I'll never have to thwart his advances. Just be glad I specified Hal and not that fellow from the store the other day."

This was almost too much to process, but Gran did just fine. "Another beau? You're two-timing the sheriff already?"

"Gran, stop! I'm not dating the sheriff or that awful guy from the store."

The whole lot of them giggled at my expense.

Kalene went next, granting me enhanced potion-making. She was even less foresighted than Hilda, not realizing that she would lose some of her potion-making skills for the whole of the year, a skill, that as I understood, wasn't strong in the first place.

Lauren attempted to ease that burden, also granting me skill in potion-making.

Finally, it was Gran's turn.

"As your blood relative and the head of this makeshift assembly, I have the ability to grant you something a little more powerful than the others. Something a little more nebulous. I grant you the ability to see trouble before it sees you."

I felt something flow through me. It was nothing like the burning of Agatha's gift, more a tingle. Everyone pulled their hand from the tree, including me.

"What does that even mean? Like precognition?"

Gran smiled cheekily. "You'll just have to find out."

"She always talks like that," Trish confided. "The enchantments have to be really specific. Usually, at least. We can't grant you protection from an evildoer because, well, none of us are protected like that. But Hilda, she's been building immunity to poisons her whole life."

"I eat four roots and three berries every morning with my coffee," Hilda interrupted. "Started with one root and half a berry twenty-eight years ago."

"And I naturally thwart men," Trish said. "Been doing it since middle school."

I chuckled. "I'm going to save my praise until I know it's working."

"You won't have to wait long," Trish said. "You'll be seeing him tomorrow."

"I will?"

She nodded. "Yep. I'm supposed to deliver a message. We're meeting at the store Monday morning—we get to find out our and the store's fate."

16

IN WITCH WE LEARN WHO'S THE BOSS?

We convened the next morning at the front of the store, between the cash registers and the aisles. We had just enough space for all of the employees. Workers from all shifts, some I'd yet to meet, and others I knew, like Trish. Hal was there too.

He made a beeline for me, muttering to himself, like when he put his number in my phone. That was a phone call I'd never be making.

Just when I thought Trish's protection spell didn't work, Hal stopped abruptly and went the other way.

Whew. That was one bullet dodged. Now, to see what this meeting was all about.

"All right, now. Let's quiet down." Sheriff Marsters—Dave—stood between my and Trish's registers, addressing the throng of Caulfield Grocery employees. "I know you're wondering what's going on, and why you're here. And probably who the heck this guy is."

Dave pointed at Cyrus Tadros, the man Trish and I met the day I discovered Mr. Caulfield's body.

Cyrus, who'd nodded along with Dave's words, kept

nodding, apparently expecting the sheriff to give more of an introduction.

Dave looked at him expectantly.

"Oh, that's my cue?" Cyrus asked.

Dave grunted.

Maybe I was reading too much into things, but something was off. The way they eyed each other showed tension between them. But whether it was about the murder or something else, I wasn't sure.

I nudged Trish and tried to whisper a question.

She shushed me before I got anything out. "*Shh*. I want to hear this."

"I guess that's my cue," Cyrus said. "That's one way to do it. Not exactly what I would've done, but anyway... What the sheriff was trying to say is I have the answers you're waiting for.

"First off, you're probably wondering if you still have a job. The answer to that question is yes—yes, you all have jobs at Caulfield Grocery."

He cleared his throat. "Now, Mr. Caulfield didn't have any relatives. He never made a will and his estate will have to be settled by a court, which will almost certainly take years. But the city council was concerned and petitioned for a temporary executor to be appointed. My name was suggested—"

"By you," Dave said, loud enough for everyone to hear.

"Right, well, I did see this as an opportunity," Cyrus replied primly. "Not only financially, I think this might be a great way of getting to know the community outside of the vineyard."

"The vineyard?" someone from the peanut gallery asked.

"Oh, that's right. *Real* introductions." He glared at Dave, who was on his way out. "My name is Cyrus Tadros. My father was Edward Armand—the owner of Armand Vineyards."

There were a few nods and some mumbling.

Scanning the crowd, I took stock of everyone. I saw a few shocked faces. Maybe, like me, they didn't know the vineyard was still operational.

Jade Gerwig, the butcher, was glaring at me. She held my eyes until I was so uncomfortable I had to look away. And when I looked back, her beady black eyes were still locked on mine. A chill ran down my spine.

A faded memory rang warning bells in my head. I remembered Jade's fight, or argument, or whatever with Mr. Caulfield the day before his murder.

Mr. Caulfield had wanted Jade back that night. She said she wasn't going to make it.

What if she did?

Cyrus went on, "I understand that Dad and Eric, that is, Mr. Caulfield, had a bit of a rough history. It's something I don't know much about. I'm hoping to make things right by keeping both of their legacies intact.

"As a few of you know," his eyes went to Trish and me, "I didn't grow up here in Creel Creek. I only saw Dad a few times. But I'm happy to be here now. And I'm happy to keep this place going. That is, with your help."

With *our* help seemed right. I wondered how he thought he was going to run the grocery store and his father's vineyard slash winery. While I'd had my disagreements with Mr. Caulfield and how he ran things, the grocery store was his life. He'd been here all hours of the day. From what I'd seen of the vineyard, Cyrus had his work cut out for him there.

How is he going to manage both?

"Over the next few hours," he said, "we'll need to clear out anything that might've spoiled or gone out of date over the past couple of days. It won't be much, but I want the whole store tended to while I conduct interviews with a few individuals about some newly open positions. Does that sound fair?"

More murmurs.

So, he's going to promote from within—a solid business practice.

I wished Dave was still there, I needed to tell him about Jade.

But I also wanted to say something to him, something not about murder or groceries.

Remember—you're not divorced yet, I reminded myself. And Dave came with baggage. Cute baggage, like designer luggage.

Cyrus was giving us that expectant look again.

Hal was the first to come to Cyrus's aid. "We should start with the milk," he said. "And there'll be some spoiled produce, for sure."

"Sounds good." Cyrus nodded his approval. "If you'll take the milk, I'm sure Nick and his crew can handle the produce. That reminds me, we'll have a truck to unload tomorrow morning. I want us open on time, if possible. This town needs their groceries."

"Very possible!" Hal's chipper voice was like a salute.

Everyone went to work.

"Constance," Cyrus waved me over, "I'd like to speak with you first, if I may."

"Sure." I glanced at Trish for support—which she failed to offer.

"He likes you," she said.

"But we don't like him," I whispered.

"We? I thought you were on *his* side the other day."

"Not anymore."

Trish smiled. "Then don't do anything I wouldn't do."

Cyrus led me to the breakroom. He shuddered—so did I—as we passed Mr. Caulfield's office. While I was glad not to have this meeting there, I also wondered why it would give *him* the creeps. Surely it had been cleaned after Mr. Caulfield's death. *Undeath*?

Cyrus closed the door behind us.

"Do you know why I wanted to talk with you?" he asked.

"Honestly, I don't."

He smiled. "You were surprised to see me this morning. It was written all over your face. After the way we met, you're probably a little suspicious of me—the way I've inserted myself into your town. I wouldn't blame you if you are."

I shrugged. "It's not my town. But yes, it is a tad convenient. We run into you the day of the murder and now here you are, in charge of this place. My new boss."

"Trust me, Constance, it's anything but convenient. I don't want to be here just as much as you don't want me here. However, it's what's best for the city. And that's what matters right now."

"I never said I didn't want you—"

"You didn't have to say it." He held up his hand to shush me. "You're telling me right now—again, with your face. Your attitude. Like your friend Trish when I stepped into her shop."

"All right," I snapped. "That still doesn't tell me why you called me in here. I do still have a job, right?"

"You do. I looked at your file. You've had quite a few jobs. Really good ones. All before you turned forty."

Just before, I thought. And as of today, that point was moot. I'd turned that dreaded corner. I was over the hill.

"Many of your previous positions include some type of

management—both people and products. Now, do you see what I'm getting at?"

"I'm sorry, but I don't."

"Management, Constance. I'm trying to give you a job. A new one."

"Wait. I thought—"

"You thought *I* was going to run this place? No. No." He shook his head. "I have way too much going on at the vineyard. I can't run this place too. I'd really like to leave it in *your* capable hands."

"My hands? Didn't you see that I was fired from my last job?"

"The article I read said your firing was discriminatory and you probably had a solid chance at a lawsuit."

"And how does that qualify me for this job? Software and grocery stores aren't exactly the same thing."

"No, you're right, they're not," he agreed. "Should I give the job to someone else?"

I thought of Trish. She'd worked here longer. She ran her own bookstore. Plus, she could use the salary boost.

I wasn't planning on staying here long. I needed to learn more magic, learn more about the Faction, and try to find my mom. I didn't want this responsibility on top of that.

If Trish wanted the job, I wanted it to be hers.

"There's someone who would be much better than me," I told him.

"Who—Trish?" He shook his head when I nodded mine. "Heavens, no. You remember how she treated me in her store, don't you? She's not a person I'd put in charge. No, I have other options. Jade, for instance."

I gaped at him.

"You know, Jade… the butcher?"

17

PARANORMAL PODCASTS

Later that afternoon, Brad, Stevie, and I made our way to Bewitched Books to hang out with Trish and Twinkie. I'd never seen Stevie go anywhere outside the neighborhood and was surprised by his offer to tag along.

The three familiars were immediately off doing familiar things. They were like kids needing to go outside and play.

"What do they do when they go off like that?" I asked Trish.

She shrugged. "Play in the shadow realm. Speak that gobbledygook to each other."

"Oh." I'd expected something more interesting.

"Now, are you going to tell me what Cyrus wanted with you or what?"

I gave Trish a rundown of my talk with Cyrus.

"I thought I told you not to do anything I wouldn't do," Trish said. "I would totally have taken that gig."

"That's kind of the problem," I said. "I thought he'd give *you* the job if I didn't take it."

"Seriously? After the other day? What were you thinking? Oh snap. He didn't give the store to Hal, did he?"

"Not Hal."

"Nick?" she guessed.

"Not Nick."

"Then who?"

"Jade," I said with some trepidation.

Trish didn't pick up on it. "Oh, I guess that's a solid choice."

"Is it?" I asked, deciding not to say anything about the death stare she was giving me during the meeting. "I was thinking. Where was she the morning I, uh, you know…"

"When you *found* the body?"

"I'm being serious," I said, realizing Trish wasn't picking up my vibes. "And what about the night before? I heard her and Mr. Caulfield in his office fighting. He wanted her to be back at work that night."

"And?"

"And she said she couldn't come."

"That probably means she didn't," Trish said. "Come on. There's absolutely no way she did it. She's sweet. Plus, there's not a magical bone in her body. Remember, we're dealing with someone who made daylight."

Trish was sorting through a bin of dropped off books. Someone had donated their stash of Eighties romances, complete with Fabio covers. I picked one up. The yellowed pages felt brittle.

"I remember," I said. "I know a lot more about daylight now. Gran had to make some for Dave. It's nasty stuff. She left a cauldron to ferment in the downstairs bathroom. It's like we're homebrewing beer."

"Weird," Trish said. "What's Dave going to use it for?"

"For some sort of testing." I shrugged, feeling like we hadn't fully explored my suspicions about Jade.

I grabbed another book and put it in Trish's keep pile, a favorite from my reading too much romance phase. I could never work in a bookstore. I'd want to keep them all.

Trish inspected the book. "This cover is creepy looking."

"You should know not to judge a—"

"I'm going to stop you there." Trish put up a hand. "There's a reason books have covers. And it's to judge them. And this one is creepy."

"Creepy," I repeated, the gears of my mind shifting. "Hey. What if she found out?"

"Who?" Trish questioned.

"Jade," I said.

"About?"

"About Mr. Caulfield!"

"You've got to warn me when you change topics like that," Trish said. "Even if Jade knew, she'd still need a witch or a magic book to make the potion."

"There's plenty of witches around here," I said. "How well do we really know them? What if that Lauren girl is besties with Jade? What then?"

Trish considered that. "I guess you're right. Dave did ask me about everyone when he was in here yesterday. What—why are you looking at me like that?"

"I'm not looking at you any kind of way."

"Constance! Yes, you are. If I didn't know any better, I'd think you really do have a crush on Dave Marsters. And you're jealous he came over here."

"I'm not jealous," I said defensively. "It's not like I have the hots for him. I just think he's nice."

"Okay, that's a lie," Trish said. "You definitely have the hots for him."

"I mean he *is* weirdly cute." I sighed.

"I guess," she agreed. "If you're into his type."

"The hunk of manly man with a lot of chest hair type?"

"The man type." She waited for my floundering brain to catch up.

"Oh! Oh... Really?" That hadn't even occurred to me.

"Don't worry. You're not my type either."

"Thanks. Or not thanks?"

"Oh, don't be offended," she said. "You're too tall for me. But see, there's nothing to be jealous about. I just had some information that you don't. You only met a few witches the other night. There's a lot more in the area, and they all use this shop."

I was finally able to be honest with myself. Trish was right. Jealousy had snuck up on me. I was jealous of her. Jealous of Gran. I needed to think about something else. Well, I had my powers now, maybe I should start using them. "I just wish I could be more help," I said.

"Babe, you're a novice witch with no education. How much help do you think you can be?"

I shrugged.

Trish rolled her eyes. "I'll be sure to include you next time he sends me out on a secret mission. Now, tell me why you think Jade could be our culprit?"

I told her about the meeting. Jade knew that I knew—I was privy to her spat with Mr. Caulfield. I needed to tell Dave.

"Or maybe she thinks it's you," Trish countered.

"I don't know. I think that'd be worse. Why would anyone think it was me?"

"It's pretty common knowledge you didn't like him."

"Really?"

"It's all right. It's not like she knows you're a witch. And she didn't know anything about Mr. Caulfield, either."

Trish's reassurance didn't work. "No. That's what I was trying to say. What if she *did*?"

"You keep saying that. I don't see how she could have—"

"Have you heard of *Creel Creek After Dark*?" I asked.

"Of what?"

"It's a podcast."

"I've heard of podcasts," Trish said. "I'm not into them. Wait. Did you say Creel Creek?"

I nodded. "Well, I *am* into them. And I found this one—it's about us. About paranormals, that is. The good thing is the rest of the country probably thinks it's a joke. But maybe it's kind of real."

"You know it's real."

I shook my head. "I'm not sure if the hosts know it's real."

"Who are they?"

"They use pseudonyms. Silly ones. Athena Hunter and Ivana Stake."

"Ivana Stake? Or Ivana Steak? That could be Jade."

"I know. That's what I was thinking."

"When did you start thinking it?" Trish asked.

"Just a minute ago."

Trish laughed. "You're telling me you hadn't put that together until now?"

"I think I had, on some level," I protested.

"The lower level." She grinned. "I'd bet money the other host is Summer Shields."

"I thought she was a reporter."

"Side gigs." Trish motioned at her stack of books. "We've all got 'em. The question is, do they really know anything, or are they spouting nonsense?"

"We can listen to one, if you want."

At that moment, there was a rustling of feet. Many sets of feet. Then something smashed into a bookshelf, hard. Several books toppled from their shelves.

"Ouch," Brad's sonorous voice said.

A second later, Twinkie scurried across the bookstore with Stevie in hot pursuit.

"What's going on?" Trish asked.

"Stevie's gone native," Twinkie gasped, scurrying up Trish's leg. Soon, there was a tangle of cat twisted around her ankles.

"My bad," Stevie said, as if coming to. "The shadow realm always does that to me. I should've warned you."

"Lucky I was able to run interference," Brad said, rubbing at the back of his head.

"What were you doing in the shadow realm?" I asked.

"Playing shadow tag," Twinkie offered. "It keeps us on our A game. And Brad had never played."

"The second we returned," Brad said, "this one went full cat mode."

"I'm sorry," Stevie bellowed. "It won't happen again."

"Too right, it won't." The mouse, whose head had emerged from Trish's cleavage, hunkered back down.

Brad gave me a shrug. If anything, he was as far from native raccoon as possible.

"I guess we should get going."

"No." Trish shook her head. "I want to hear this podcast. I need to see if they're outing us to the whole town."

I went into the Podcasts app on my phone and scrolled. "Let's listen to this one—it's about the murder."

Trish nodded enthusiastically. "We'll know if it's Jade in a few seconds. I've heard her voice a thousand times. You've got me a little uneasy about your theory, but I still don't think Jade would hurt a fly."

"She's a butcher," I said. "She carves animals for a living."

"Not while they're alive."

"What about Summer?" I asked. "Exposing a story like this could put her on the map."

"But it didn't," Trish argued. "There was barely a news story."

"I didn't mean the news story." I held up the phone. "I meant the podcast. At ten thousand listens and counting."

18

CREEL CREEK AFTER DARK EPISODE 45

IT'S GETTING LATE.

Very late.
The creeping dread of tomorrow haunts your dreams.
It's dark out. Are you afraid?
Welcome to Creel Creek After Dark.

Athena: I'm your host Athena Hunter. With me, as always, is the lovely Ivana Steak.

Ivana: That's right, I'm Ivana Steak. And I'm totally lovely. Except I'm not quite up there with our host Athena.

Athena: Aw, you're too kind.

Ivana: Welcome to the show where we cut deep into the strange happenings, stranger people, and even weirder history of Virginia's spookiest town, Creel Creek.

Athena: This is an odd episode.

Ivana: Aren't they all?

Athena: What I meant to say, before I was so rudely interrupted, is this is an *unplanned* episode. Next week, we'll be back to our normal schedule. It's almost time for the one we've been talking about forever. The vineyard episode is coming, people. Be prepared.

Ivana: I think our listeners might want to know why their ears are subject to this *unplanned* episode.

Athena: Because of this week's *strange* happening. I'm not sure I'd even call it a happening. Definitely strange. And more of a tragedy, wasn't it?

Ivana: Yes, a tragedy. We're sorry if we're not our usual snarky selves.

Athena: Are you calling me snarky, Ivana?

Ivana: No, Athena, I called *us* snarky. But yes, you're the snarkiest snark to ever snarkle in Snark Lake.

Athena: Snarkle in Snark Lake? Did you come up with that yourself?

Ivana: Again, no, Athena, you wrote that into the script to prove your snarkiness. leaving it up to me to right this ship and get us back on course.

Athena: Oh, right, I did.

Ivana: I guess that leaves it up to me to right this ship and get us back on course.

Athena: The tragedy.

Ivana: Yes, the tragedy.

Athena: We have it on good authority that the vampire—the Creel Creek Bloodsucker himself—is no longer with us.

Ivana: That's right. You'll recall our discussion of the Creel Creek Bloodsucker in episode fifteen. Well, there's evidence that this vampire had lived in our little town for over a hundred and fifty years, under different aliases.

Athena: And just recently we learned who the Bloodsucker was. Photographic proof can be seen on our website.

Athena: Now Ivana, can you remind the audience again why we call him the Bloodsucker?

Ivana: Well, apart from one killing in 1912 attributed to blood loss, there have been no deaths linked to the Bloodsucker. It was the 1950s when things got truly interesting. That's when plastic bags began to be used for blood storage. And our hospital's supply ran low. After a search, they found bags in the basement, empty, with two holes punctured in each.

Athena: As if someone sucked the blood out of the bags.

Ivana: Exactly.

Athena: But how do we know this person—the person who died—was the Bloodsucker?

Ivana: We know because we know how to spot a vampire. There are several characteristics common to all vampires and the Bloodsucker had them all.

Athena: And we have this on what authority?

Ivana: Mine.

Athena: That's pretty good authority.

Ivana: I thought so too.

Athena: But I do have a question. Can the undead really die?

Ivana: I wasn't exactly sure, not until this week.

Athena: Okay, so vampires can be killed. Do we know who killed him?

Ivana: Again no. But I know what you're going to say...

Athena: Because you have the script?

Ivana: Well, that too. But no, I didn't slay the vampire.

Athena: Me either. No matter what my last name is—I would never.

Ivana: Not even if he'd cornered you in a dark alley?

Athena: I mean, maybe. But that's totally off topic. Granted, it does make a good segue for today's show sponsor.

Purse Stakes are mini wooden stakes that fit easily in your purse and are great protection from vampires or other night stalkers. Grip and press hard into the perpetrator's chest. Find them at Purse Stakes dot net.

Ivana: Is that a real thing, Athena?

Athena: I guess you'll have to Yahoogle it and find out.

Ivana: You're always making me Yahoogle things when I prefer Goohoo.

Athena: Goohoo dot com—the world's trusted source for screening your next employee.

Ivana: Okay, now we're seriously off topic. We hope you enjoyed this special episode of *Creel Creek After Dark*. Check the show notes for more information. Hit the like or subscribe button. And remember to tune in next week!

19

IN WITCH I'M ACCUSED

We ruminated on the podcast for a little while, wondering what authority—what information Ivana, I mean Jade—it was obviously Jade—had about Mr. Caulfield.

But the more we talked about it, the more we believed they were just blowing smoke. They had good instincts, but the podcast was a joke. Even the comments section treated it that way. No one took them seriously. Maybe we didn't have anything to worry about.

Still, the next day, I tried to stay off of Jade's radar. She was busy in her new role as manager. I took my post next to Trish, hoping I could ride out the day without making any waves.

I had only been there for an hour when the intercom crackled. It squealed, piercing my and the customers' ears. There was some fumbling on the mic before Jade's voice found it.

"Constance to the manager's office," she said. "Constance Campbell to the manager's office."

Is this high school? Her tone told me all I needed to know. I was in trouble.

"Is she serious?" I asked Trish. My line was three people deep and Trish's was no better. Jade had a view of the registers from the television in Mr. Caulfield's office. She could've picked a better time to air out whatever grievance she had with me.

I continued to ring up a frumpy middle-aged woman. And after that, I started ringing up the next customer, a man.

The intercom crackled with static. "*Now*, Constance."

"I guess she means now," Trish said.

"I got that." I turned the aisle's light off. "Sir, do you mind moving to the other register?"

"But I—"

"I know," I said, shaking my head at him mournfully. "I'm sorry, but she *did* say now."

The man snorted. "Yeah, I heard her."

Jade's thin frame was dwarfed by Mr. Caulfield's desk chair. The chair was massive, filling the whole space between Mr. Caulfield's desk—her desk now—and a filing cabinet. Behind her, a coffeemaker on the cabinet was gathering dust.

I stopped in the door like that high schooler afraid to go in the principal's office. I waited for Jade to acknowledge me.

"Come in and close the door," she said without looking up.

Jade was antsy; she tapped her fingers on the desk.

"I don't want this to be awkward," she said.

Too late.

"I know you interviewed for this job. Cyrus told me. And I want you to know that just because you didn't get it, doesn't mean you aren't welcome on my team."

It probably wasn't the best time to tell her I'd actually gotten the job, I just didn't want it.

"I'd also like you to know," she went on, "that I'm not like everyone else in town. I don't jump to conclusions. I need hard evidence, facts, before I make a decision."

Now, she had me confused. *What kind of conclusions? Is everyone in town talking about me behind my back? Surely not.*

"Of course, I would love to hear it from you," she said. "Where you were the night Mr. Caulfield was killed. Trust me. I know he had enemies. But your little spat the day before, well, it does make me wonder whether or not I can trust you."

"Wait... what?"

My spat?

I had to give it to her. She didn't pull any punches. She'd just come right out and accused me. Something I couldn't have done to her. Until now.

"Are you asking if I killed Mr. Caulfield?"

"It's a simple question," she said. "I assume you can answer it, can't you?"

"Yes."

"Yes, you killed him or yes, you can answer it?"

"I meant no."

"Now I'm confused."

"Join the party," I said. "The answer is no. No—I didn't kill him. And yes, I could answer your question. But I won't."

"You're on thin ice as it is, Constance. You're sure you can't tell me where you were the night he was killed?"

"I could ask the same of you," I pointed out. "You didn't even come in that morning. And I heard your fight with him about coming in the night he was murdered."

"I'd hardly call it a fight. We had a disagreement about scheduling."

"Same with me," I argued. "I came in late that morning. Getting reprimanded by my boss is hardly a motive for murder."

"I agree," she said. "But there's something strange about you. You're different. Care to tell me why?"

Jade's words lit a fire in the pit of my stomach. Anything I said now was going to come out with venom.

"I don't know what you mean. Don't come at me with accusations when you can't even defend yourself."

"So that's how you're going to play this? Tit for tat. Okay, I'll tell you where I was that night."

I waited. She was shaking her head like a crazy person. Back and forth. Back and forth. "I was out with a friend. All night. She was with me the whole time. Neither of us killed anyone. I was running late that morning. I'd overslept."

"That's a pretty weak alibi," I said. "Who is this friend? And what were you two doing?"

I thought I had a good idea of who that friend was. But I wanted her to tell me.

"Are you the police now?" She cocked her eyebrow mockingly. "No, that's right—you're a cashier at a grocery store. I gave my friend's name and a recording of what we were doing to the *authorities*. Sheriff Marsters was happy with my explanation. I think you should be too."

I was sure she was going to tell me about her little podcast. After all, she'd gone this far. I knew she was proud of it.

"Now, do you have something to tell me?"

"Still nothing," I said.

Jade glowered at me. "Go back to your register. There seems to be a bit of a line."

I craned my neck to see the television on the side of her desk. Sure enough, it gave the manager—Mr. Caulfield included—a bird's eye view of the front of the store. Trish's line spilled out and down of the row of registers.

"That is quite a line," I said. "And if you don't want to tell me about your podcast, that's fine."

"You—you're a listener?" She struggled with that for a moment, eyes wide.

"Occasionally." I beamed at her.

"What I do in my off hours is—"

"Is fun?" I gave no indication that I thought *Creel Creek After Dark* was serious in any way.

She flushed. "Right."

And I'd been dismissed. I retreated from the office, pushing my luck by saying, "Good chat. We should do it again soon."

20

IN WITCH I GET ROBBED

Not much had changed for me since coming into my abilities. Using magic proved tricky. I'd tried a handful of spells, but I could count on no fingers how many had been successful.

Oh, I usually made *something* happen—heat coursed from my fingertips and electricity crackled through the air. But my intention always got lost in translation. I was like Luke getting stung by the training ball, not yet ready to connect with the Force.

A few days passed. Then a week. It felt good to be back to the daily grind. For the first time ever, there were customers waiting at the door every day, almost like they'd come to appreciate their local grocery.

Jade took her new role as manager seriously. She hired her replacement at the butcher counter. A hire from within —Nick, from produce, took over. Hal moved up to take Nick's place.

Jade had also promoted someone to assistant manager. This, I was less enthusiastic about. Trish took the post and in turn made me lead cashier.

I didn't let the promotion or the $0.25 an hour increase go to my head.

I was thankful for Trish's gift. Hal had neither spoken a word to nor approached me since my birthday. He chose instead to watch me from afar. I guess warding off infatuations wasn't something her protection spell could do.

The next Saturday morning, my line flowed like the conveyor belt. One in. One out. Two in. Two out. And by lunchtime, Trish had to call in more baggers. The freckle-faced youngster at the end of my register was named Craig.

And speaking of infatuations, Craig's was on the other register.

Wynter, a night shift cashier filling in this morning, had all the youth and fresh good looks of a prom queen.

"I'm going on break," she said. She had a dreamy manner of speaking, and she hardly made eye contact with anyone except Craig.

"Have fun," I said

"Yeah, have fun," Craig managed to say.

She wasn't gone long before my line got out of hand.

I rang the customers up on autopilot, chipping away at the line. I'd finally cleared it when the lights flickered off then back on again like there was a brief power outage. If the power was off for more than five minutes, the generator would kick on.

"That was weird," I said.

I glanced outside, and my eyes locked onto a man in a green hoodie. Ducking his head, he entered through the sliding doors and turned, never giving me a chance to see his face.

It was the hoodie that stood out to me. It wasn't cold. Far from it. We still had most of the summer ahead of us. A customer appeared, and then two more.

"What was?" Craig reached for a paper bag and shook it open.

I started ringing up groceries. "The lights," I said. "The way they flickered."

Craig cocked his head. "Did they?"

"I think so."

He shrugged it off. "Maybe I had my eyes closed. It wouldn't be the first time I napped on the job." He smiled. "Don't tell Jade. Or Trish."

"Have you seen Jade?" I asked him.

"This morning, maybe." He heaved a heavy bag into the customer's cart. "I think she's busy doing *manager* things." He made air quotes.

"You don't approve of manager things?"

"If she's like Mr. Caulfield, she's sitting back there drinking coffee and watching us do the work."

"Yeah?" I tried to hide my smile. That did sound accurate.

Craig lowered his voice. "I heard you got offered the job."

"Did you?" I raised my eyebrows, giving him one of those *maybe I did, maybe I didn't* smiles.

"And you turned it down?"

"Listen," I said, "I know when you're sixteen, running a store like this might seem like a decent gig. But I'm in a weird place in my life right now."

A really weird place. In life, in love, and work, I thought. And that was without adding magic to the mix.

"I'm eighteen," Craig corrected. "And I'm with you. I wouldn't touch that job either—even if it came with a six-figure salary. It doesn't come with a six-figure salary, does it?"

"I didn't ask."

He nodded, his curiosity sated for the time being. "You mind if I take my lunch too?"

"Are you and Wynter friends?" I asked.

"Not exactly." He blushed.

"She *is* cute," I told him. "I mean if you like that whole homecoming court, *Jack and Diane* thing she's got going."

"Jack and who?"

"Forget about it."

"She reminds me of the girl that used to babysit me when I was little," he said wistfully. "But no girl could ever live up to Miss Kenzi."

"Someday one will," I said.

Craig was still young. He had time to figure these things out. *Unlike me.* Silently, I wished him good luck. Then I realized that maybe I could do more than that.

Then again, my powers could backfire… on him.

He's eighteen, I reminded myself. *There will be plenty of girls.*

I thought about everything Gran had taught me so far, the little that she had. And I made a rhyme.

"Lucky in love.
Come push or shove.
If Craig deserves a mate.
Make Wynter see he's great."

Like Gran, I twirled my finger down where no one could see, and I felt the warmth of magic, that tingle that came with using my powers, flow from my fingertip.

Pleased with myself, I checked out a few more customers and found mister green hoodie next in line.

He picked up a bag of candy and set it on the belt. He

didn't have any other groceries. And when I greeted him, he ignored me. He didn't even look my way.

Not that he was the first person with odd tendencies to come through my line. Or the first one with bad wardrobe choices. Earlier that day, I'd rung up a seventy-year-old woman with a purple thong rising from her jeans.

But something about him wasn't right.

Are my powers trying to warn me?

I was glad he only had the one item.

Except there was a gun in my face before I had time to scan his M&Ms.

"ALL THE MONEY IN THE REGISTER," he muttered. His voice wasn't familiar, but the way he dragged out the syllables was.

He kept his head down, not letting me get a good look at his face.

But the only thing I was looking at was that gun. Inches away from my face. I could see every detail—most notably, the small barrel. One wrong move and a projectile moving faster than the speed of sound would rocket out of it and through my witchy skull.

I wondered if this guy knew how little money was left in the drawers—a few hundred dollars, tops.

"Is three hundred dollars worth killing someone for?" I whispered.

"Shut up," he shouted. "Open the till."

It was his voice that drew the attention of the entire store, not mine.

He noticed it too. A woman down the cereal aisle pulled out her phone. The robber moved his gun from me to her.

"Put the phone down," he demanded. "Everyone get down! Slide your phones this way."

The sound of phones skittering against the floor was surreal. A still lit phone stopped beside his foot. The woman's phone had dialed out, there was a call on the line.

The thief bent down to end it.

That was probably the moment I should have done something. I should've used my magic.

After all, I'd just performed a spell—and one that maybe had worked. At least, nothing had backfired.

These were the kind of circumstances where magic was useful. It was just me who was useless. I was petrified.

Green hoodie thief turned back to the register, frustrated. His eyes went wide. "Where'd she go?"

He swung the gun around, looking around wildly then he leaned over to get a better look under the register. The gun waved around, nearly connecting with my head. I shied away.

"Where the hell did she go?"

No one in the store offered him an answer. I was speechless, waiting for one of them to point and say, "She's right there, doofus."

He looked again, sweeping the space behind the register with the gun. It should've clocked me right in the head. But it passed through me like I wasn't there at all.

I looked down and realized that I *wasn't* there at all. My hands, my arms, my body, none of me was visible. I screamed, or I would have. Except my voice had also disappeared.

I watched, dumbstruck, as the agitated thief gave up looking for me and went for what he hoped was a payday. He pounded on the register, but everything needs a password these days. Too bad for him.

Sirens sounded in the distance. Green hoodie looked up, and I finally caught a glimpse of his face. He was younger than Craig by a hair—the peach fuzz kind on his chin. His blue eyes were panicked.

Now was the time for him to run. He hadn't stolen anything yet, although waving a gun was a serious enough crime. He grabbed the M&Ms and made a break for it.

Except instead of running out the doors and into the parking lot, he bolted the other way—through the store, sidestepping around people on the floor and dodging their buggies.

Two sheriff's vehicles pulled up in the fire lane. One familiar SUV, one cruiser. Dave and Willow burst from their vehicles. They drew their weapons, then Dave indicated for Willow to go around the building while he took the front of the store.

The doors slid open and Dave entered, searching for the threat. Like the green hoodie M&M thief, he looked through me to Trish, who'd been down one of the aisles.

"That way," she mouthed, pointing energetically.

Nodding, Dave moved stealthily in that direction. When he was out of my line of sight I turned my gaze outside to where their vehicles were parked, sirens off but lights spinning.

To my surprise, I saw a person out there.

He'd stripped off the green hoodie. With his baggy jeans sliding off, the thief jogged to a rusty old Cavalier and peeled out of the parking lot.

"He got away!" Trish yelled. "Did you see that?"

I realized she was talking to me. I looked down to see that I was solid once again. I hadn't noticed it happen. And I was hoping no customers had either.

From their vantage point on the ground, it probably looked like I was ducking under my register the whole time.

"I saw," I said.

"Dave!" Trish shouted. "Where are you? He just got away."

"We have other problems," Dave called back. "Get over here."

I followed Trish to the meat counter where Dave was kneeling over a body, two fingers on the side of its neck. I moved to get a better look at the body's owner. He wore jeans and a vest like mine.

Hal.

Dave sighed. He shook his head, then spoke into the radio on his shoulder.

"Dispatch, are EMTs in route?"

A garbled response.

"No," he replied. "No shots fired. We have one in need of assistance. I think he just fainted."

As Dave spoke, Hal's eyes fluttered open.

"You all right there, big fella?" Dave asked.

Hal nodded. "What... what happened?"

Nick, who was standing a few feet away behind the counter, said, "That kid passed us on his way out. You saw the gun, and the next thing I know, your eyes rolled into your head and you hit the deck. Hard."

"How hard?"

Nick fought a smile. "Pretty hard."

"All right, well, wait here," Dave told Hal. "We'll get you checked out for concussion."

By this time, the whole store had regrouped around the butcher counter. Willow hovered at the edge of the crowd. She looked upset, but she tried to get Dave's attention without anyone else noticing.

"What happened to you?" he asked. "You let him get away?"

"Not exactly," she said without elaborating.

Dave scratched the stubble on his cheeks, frustrated by how the events had played out.

This was my third encounter with the sheriff's office. It was the most stressful yet. Granted, the suspect had only gotten away with a bag of M&Ms. Still, he'd pointed a gun at my face.

Dave sighed and held up his hands. "Let's interview the main witnesses. Get everyone else's information and cut them loose."

"You aren't going after him?" Trish asked.

Dave glared at her. "Tell me what he got away with first."

"M&Ms," I said.

"Then no, Trish, we're *not* going after him. We'll look at the video and try to identify him. We're going to need your breakroom again. Whose register did he try to rob?"

"Who do you think?" Trish pointed at me.

"Of course," Dave said. "And where's Jade?"

"The bank, I think."

"Well, I hope she's not robbing it," Dave joked.

In the breakroom, I told him what happened—everything, including when I vanished or whatever that was. He didn't say much, just nodded and scribbled notes. Willow and Trish sat on the counter behind us.

Dave leaned back in his chair. "You going to tell us how you let him get away?" he asked Willow when I'd finished.

"I had a vision," she said meekly. "I had him covered when he came out the door. I told him to stop. Then I wasn't *here* anymore."

"Not here?" Trish asked.

"She freezes up," Dave replied. "Her eyes get cloudy and

she goes stiff. It's freaky. But I imagine Constance going incorporeal is freaky too."

"What was this vision?" Trish asked Willow.

"It was us," Willow said. "The four of us, I mean."

"Were we in a breakroom?" I asked.

"No." She shook her head. "At Nell Baker's cabin."

"Why on Earth would we be at Nell Baker's cabin?" Dave asked. "And who is Nell Baker?"

"It has something to do with Mr. Caulfield's murder."

"Okay," Trish said slowly. "There's just one problem. None of us know where Nell Baker lives."

"That's right," Willow agreed. "We don't. But she can find out."

I was surprised to find Willow's finger pointed in my direction.

There was a knock on the breakroom door. Dave answered it.

Jade stood there, a scowl creasing her normally smooth forehead. "I leave for fifteen minutes and this is what I come back to? What the heck happened?"

"A robbery," Dave said. "But not much of one. I'm sure one of your other employees can fill you in."

"Why not you? Or them?" She gestured at me and Trish.

"Because I need to take them with me. Police business. I'm sure you understand."

Jade glared in my direction with a triumphant glint in her eye, like all her suspicions about me had been confirmed.

21

IN WITCH WE FIND THE CABIN IN THE WOODS

"You didn't have to say it like that." I climbed into the passenger seat of Dave's SUV—not the back as Jade would've liked. Trish got in the car with Willow.

"Like what?" Dave asked.

"Like I'm wanted for questioning in Mr. Caulfield's murder," I said. "Jade already thinks I did it."

"She does?"

I bobbed my head up and down wearily as I fastened my seatbelt.

"Don't take it personally," Dave said. "Jade is suspicious of everyone and everything. You've really got to be careful around her."

"I've noticed," I said. Dave knew about the podcast from her alibi—if he wasn't already a listener.

"Her podcast sheds a certain light on our little town," I said. "I'd like to know what she was recording the night of Mr. Caulfield's death."

"She told you about her alibi?" he asked.

"Yes." I stretched the truth a little.

"Why would she tell you that?" he asked. "Who was sleuthing? You or her?"

"Both," I admitted. Now he sounded like I was butting into the case when he was the one who needed *my* help.

"She accused me, so I accused her. Please, just tell me what she was doing."

"I can't really say."

"It *is* about her podcast, *Creel Creek After Dark*, isn't it?"

"It is."

It took me and Trish the better part of an afternoon to figure that out.

"Then why can't you tell me? Did you listen to it?"

"No, have you?"

"A few episodes," I said. "Wait. You didn't listen?"

He shook his head. "Not yet. I haven't had time. I have a copy of it. They were up at the—"

"At the vineyard," I cut him off, knowing this had to be the episode they'd been building up to—the one they were so excited to share. And Dave had a copy of it.

Woop!

Behind us, a siren blipped. Willow and Trish were glaring in our direction. It dawned on me that we weren't moving.

"I don't know where I'm supposed to be going."

"That's right. I'm supposed to know. Except I don't know either."

"Willow said you would."

"Wood." A memory popped into my brain. The first episode of the podcast I'd listened to—the story from a listener about a cabin in a wood outside of town. A cabin where a witch lived. And died.

"It had to be Nell Baker," I said to myself.

"What had to be?"

"A cabin in a wood," I said. "I know what I have to do. Help me think of a rhyme. What rhymes with wood?"

Dave smirked. "Could, should, pould, good."

"Pould isn't a word."

Dave shrugged. "Doin' my best over here."

I racked my brain.

"She lived in a cabin in a wood.
She was a witch who wasn't good.
I need a map to her place.
So we can solve this case?"

"Is that really going to work?" Dave asked after I finished.

"I don't know."

"Starting route to *cabin in a wood*," a familiar woman's voice said.

I pulled out my phone. The map was open with a destination plugged in and directions highlighted.

"I think it worked." Dave threw the SUV into drive.

We followed the directions to the other side of town and an old dirt road not even indicated on the actual map. The highlighted route told us to turn. Dave maneuvered the SUV over bumps and craters for about a mile until the road narrowed and disappeared.

We all got out and followed the map into the woods, over a stream, and through thick brush.

The directions ended at Nell's cabin. It wasn't the well-built log structure I'd pictured in my head. It was more a shack, made of plywood and spare siding. There was a single window and a door.

Only a hundred feet or so from the stream, it was

erected in a glade just large enough for it. In fact, an oak limb brushed the tin roof like an arm over a shoulder.

"Wow," Trish said, "this is *exactly* what I imagined when I read about witches as a kid."

"I don't know," I said. "It's not what I pictured at all."

"That's because you had a real childhood. Tiffany Aching, Harry Potter—Mom told me they weren't real. I wasn't allowed to read them."

"Wait... you didn't read Harry Potter?"

"Ladies!" Dave shushed us.

It was pointless. Fallen leaves covered the ground, swishing and crunching with every step. If Nell was in there, we weren't going to surprise her.

Not that I wanted to give a witch who lived in a squalid shack like this one a fright. But neither did I want to give one much of a head start.

"I read some," Trish whispered. "And I watched the movies."

Dave sighed. "Well, there's no use being tactical with you two around. Nell Baker," he hollered at the door. "Nell Baker, if you're in there I need you to come to the door."

There was no movement from the shack. But there were sounds. The sound of animals, clawing and hissing. Shrieks peppered the noise, sounding like profanity. I couldn't tell if they were somewhere in the distance or inside.

Dave approached the door and pounded it twice. The animal sounds went absolutely nuts.

Inside, I thought.

"Nell Baker. This is the county sheriff. Please, open the door." Dave turned to Willow. "What happens next?"

"This is as far as I got."

"Are you telling me you might have led us into a trap?"

"Never once has my gift led me into trouble," Willow protested. "Well, not much trouble."

There was a rustling of leaves behind us, and we all turned to find a raccoon staring up at us, wide-eyed, his paws to his little chest.

"Brad?"

"There's nothing from the *other side* beyond that door. Nothing to worry about."

"Brad, where did you come from?"

"From your grandmother's," he said.

"Who is Brad? And why are you talking to a raccoon?"

"It's her familiar." To me, Trish said, "Dave and Willow can't understand familiars. You're going to have to translate."

"Oh," I said, intrigued by this turn of events. "He says there's nothing to worry about inside."

"That's not exactly what he said," Trish countered. "He said there's nothing from the other side to worry about in there. Probably not a witch in there either."

"Not a live one," Brad said, on tiptoes sniffing the air.

"That's right," I said to him. "You're supposed to protect me. Where were you an hour ago when I was getting robbed?"

Trish came to Brad's defense. "He can only protect you from the other side. From otherworldly things. You know, things that go bump in the night."

"You have this lot," the raccoon said, waving a paw in Dave's direction, "to protect you from everything else."

It didn't seem like Brad was impressed with our local sheriff and his deputy.

"All right. The varmint says the coast is clear. That's good enough for me." Dave kicked in the cabin door, and that's when the smell hit us.

The stench of death and animal feces threatened to

knock us into yesterday. And the animal sounds went through the roof, raising by decibels. Cages shaking, birds shrieking, a possum hissing.

Nell kept rows of cages stacked against a wall. Twelve total, each with an animal locked inside. There were snakes, squirrels, a possum, and a hawk. Some had water, but their food bowls were empty and probably had been for some time.

Then there was Nell herself, sitting quietly in a rocking chair, rotting. That story, the one they'd read on the podcast, was true. It had to be.

And that meant the story's antagonist, the one who'd come to kill Nell and to steal her book, well, they were real too.

22

THE VAMPIRE'S ESTATE

Dave called it in. It would be a while before the coroner could get out here to us.

Trish and I waited outside while Dave and Willow tried to look around inside the cabin. The smell was so intense they could only stay a minute or so before they had to come out for fresh air.

I explained the story to them—what I remembered.

"It's like you feared," Willow said to Dave. "Someone is after us."

"But she wasn't murdered," Trish protested. "Look at her. She died in her sleep. For all we know, the story was just that, a story."

"It mentions a book," I said.

"A book? What book?"

"It didn't say." I shrugged. "One that Nell owned." I was hoping that maybe Trish had sold it to her. I gave her a questioning look.

Trish shook her head. "No. She wasn't an avid shopper. I don't know what Nell kept here. But by the look of it, not much."

"That doesn't mean she didn't have an important book," I said. "Would it come to you after she passed? Your mother's spell?"

Trish looked uneasy—maybe I'd said too much.

"What's this about someone after us?" Trish changed the subject.

"You know," Dave said. "A slayer. A hunter. I didn't say there *is* one. I'm just not going to rule it out. Someone killed a vampire, after all."

"Right. Exactly," Trish snapped. "Probably just a slayer coming through town."

"A slayer?" I asked.

"Come on. I know you've seen Buffy. Whoever it was, they're probably long gone by now."

"Then why would my vision lead us here?" Willow asked. "Why would they kill a witch?"

"I'm trying to tell you they didn't kill her. Mother Nature did."

"Still, why are we out here?" Dave asked.

"Because someone had to find Nell's body," I said.

Willow began to make a perimeter with police tape. And Dave brought the animal cages out to the side of the house.

"Okay, should we let them out?" I gestured at the cages.

"I'm not sure," Trish replied. "It's not like any of them know how to live as animals."

"Not anymore?" I asked. "How long do you think they've been cooped up like that?"

"I don't think they've ever lived as animals," Trish said.

"What do you mean?" Dave asked.

"Yeah, what do you mean?"

"Don't be dense, Constance. You know *exactly* what I mean. Nell was a witch. She did *witchy* things."

"Witchy things like what?"

"Like turn people into animals," Brad suggested.

"She talked about it at one of our little get-togethers with your Gran. She claimed they were bad people."

"What kind of bad people?" Dave asked.

"I don't know. Lawyers and repo men. People from the IRS."

"You've got to be—"

"I'm just kidding." Trish slapped Dave's back. "Seriously? You believed that? Look at this place. Does this look like a place a repo man would visit? 'Ma'am, I'm going to need to take that cauldron. You're fifteen payments behind.'"

"Oh." I was glad she was joking.

"You got me." Dave whistled. "I thought these really were people."

"They are," Trish said. "That wasn't the joke."

My heart sank. *That wasn't the joke?*

"You ever see the show *Dexter*?" Trish said.

"Yeah," we chorused.

"Well… if I had to guess…"

"Something tells me you're not really guessing," Dave replied.

"Okay, you're right. My mom told me about it. She's been doing this a long time. What my mom did with books, Nell did to draw murderers and rapists to Creel Creek, into a trap. Then she did this."

I squatted down next to a possum, hissing and baring its fangs at me.

"And she kept them here in this shack?" I put my hand out to show the possum I meant him no harm. "What if they didn't come?"

A spark left my fingertip the instant I said it. It zapped the possum on the nose. The animal began to change.

First, the twitchy, whiskery possum nose and mouth

turned to lips buried in a beard, under a hawk-like nose. The spell traveled down the possum's body, changing it before our eyes until finally, the thick possum tail morphed to the hairy behind of a middle-aged man.

The cage struggled to contain him. Every inch of him was pressing against the thin metal bars. His eyes were wild and frantic. He twisted his hand toward the padlocked latch, but it was secure. The frame of the door, not so much.

"Blood," he screamed. "No blood. Let me out of here. Blood. No blood. Let me out. Let me out, you bi—"

"Do something!" Trish yelled.

"I-I—don't know how."

"Point your finger at him and repeat after me,

"Your misdeeds sealed your fate.
You're destined to be a possum in a crate."

To our amazement, it worked.

"See," Trish said, pretending she wasn't surprised herself. "It wouldn't've worked if he hadn't done some misdeeds. So, there's that."

"Everyone has misdeeds," Dave argued. "That doesn't prove he's a killer."

"Sorry if I couldn't think of a good rhyme for a killer," Trish replied.

"Thriller. Miller. Filler."

"Okay, I see your point. Let's change him back. You're welcome to ask him. Constance?"

"Why me?"

"Cause my magic won't transfigure people like that. Trust me. I've tried."

Dave smirked. "I bet you have."

The sound of crunching leaves startled us. We turned to

see Willow ducking under branches, climbing the steep hill on the other side of the cabin.

"Did I just see that possum turn into a man?" she asked.

"It's best if you don't ask," Dave replied. "We've got a big enough mess on our hands. Let's get the humane society out here. And let's forget any of this ever happened."

"I've got something I want to show you," Dave said as we climbed into his SUV.

Willow and some state troopers were taking care of the scene, letting the coroner do his job.

Trish clambered into the backseat. As soon as she closed the door, she realized there was no getting out—not without help.

"I don't like this." She tested the door. "I don't like this one bit."

"I don't know." Dave laughed, turning to me. "It seems kind of fitting, doesn't it?"

I smiled. Trish and I were getting along well. I didn't want to chance it with a bad joke.

"About as fitting as your mustache," I quipped.

"Hey, now." Dave scowled playfully, then ran his fingers along his mustache. "This is fashionable... if you're a cop."

"Or a 70s porn star," Trish added.

Dave shook his head and asked her, "Are you coming with us or should I drop you off at the bookstore?"

"Actually, I should probably get back to the grocery store. Jade needs all the help she can get."

"Make sure Hal gets a few days off," Dave said when we turned into the parking lot.

In the rearview mirror, Trish rolled her eyes in trademark fashion.

"Poor guy's been through the wringer," Dave said. "It's the least you can do after that knock on the head."

"He'll be fine," Trish said.

"Oh, stop being mean to the poor guy."

"Yeah, why are you so mean to him?" I knew why I didn't like him. But Trish bristled every time she saw him. She couldn't hide her contempt, like with Cyrus Tadros, so maybe it was a guy thing.

"Mean to him?" Trish scoffed. "I'm not *mean* to him. I just think he's gross. It's his own fault."

"How is it his own fault?" Dave asked.

"The man eats cereal for every meal—breakfast, lunch, and dinner. You know that's not healthy."

"He eats lunch in the deli," I said.

"Okay," she said, uncowed, "two meals a day."

"Two meals," I said, placating her. She may have been right. The times Hal had gone through my line, he had bought a lot of cereal—a crazy amount, usually on a buy one get one free deal.

"You can't blame him." Dave let out a sigh.

"What did you mean, he's been through the wringer?" I asked.

Dave let Trish out of the car. She waved and disappeared through the automatic doors.

"I mean Hal's had it rough." Dave jumped back into the vehicle and the conversation. "He was a loner in high school. Yes, we're the same age."

Dave had Hal beat by a good ten years on youthful good looks.

"He lived with his mom until she passed, some years

ago. I kind of lost track of him for a while, then I guess the insurance money ran out."

"You mean he hasn't worked at the grocery long?"

"About a year. Give or take."

That surprised me. Hal had an air about him, like he'd been working there forever, longer than Mr. Caulfield—which was impossible.

"You're probably wondering where I'm taking you," Dave said nonchalantly.

He kept going, turning down back roads and up side streets, into a part of town I'd never seen.

Despite its small population, Creel Creek was a geographically large and sprawling "small town." The only barriers to expansion were the trees, the distant mountains, and the utter lack of people willing to move here.

"It never occurred to me," I said candidly. "Where are you taking me?"

A part of me hoped it had nothing to do with witches or dead vampires. But that part of me also knew I was kidding myself.

"That possum back there—he said blood several times. It got me to thinking. Maybe this is all linked somehow. Not by a slayer, something else. See, both Willow and Trish have tried to conjure at the Caulfield place. You didn't have your magic yet, so I didn't bother asking. We found an odd room. You'll see. There's not much to it."

"So, you're taking me to a vampire's lair?" My hopes fell to the wayside. "What kind of odd are we talking about?"

"You'll see." Dave could see my mind spinning. "Don't worry. He didn't live in a castle on a hill or anything."

We reached a gated community and Dave punched in a code. The neighborhood behind the fence included a golf course and the nicest homes I'd seen in Creel Creek. So nice, it was hard to believe they belonged here.

The houses weren't mansions but two-story brick homes on half-acre lots, most with pools in the backyard.

We pulled in and parked at a house in a cul-de-sac. Much like the others, but the grass wasn't as green. And unlike the rest, it *did* have a turret. I smiled at that, castle or no castle.

It was late afternoon and the sun was sliding behind the mountains. It was getting darker and the house's up-lighting had clicked on.

I expected to be ushered through the front door, but Dave went around to the side.

"It's in the basement, which he walled off from the main house for some reason."

"Is there a coffin?" I asked.

"You'd think so, but no."

On this side of the house, the yard sloped down, almost level with the basement. It was only a few steps down to a storm door. Dave fiddled with keys, found the right one, and slid it into the lock.

"Brace yourself," he said.

Brace myself for what? I wondered, fully expecting a dark and dungeonlike room to do vampire things in. *Vampire things*. I rolled my eyes at myself. *What does that even mean? Drink blood?*

What I didn't expect was to shield my eyes from the blinding white light when Dave flipped the switch.

Like the lights overhead, the walls and the linoleum floors were glaringly white. The room itself had the sterile vibe of a hospital. It smelled like lemon cleaner and rubbing alcohol. It all made sense when I noticed the gurney on the other side of the room. Beside it, there were two IV infusion stands. And opposite, a table with what looked like supplies to draw blood. A deep freezer hummed somewhere.

"I wanted to preserve it as is," Dave commented. "But it's been difficult to keep other agencies out. I took one of the blood bags from the freezer and had it tested. It's human, donor unknown."

"He... he drew blood in here?" I was at a loss. I imagined a person on the gurney and a vampire jabbing them with needles, which I guess was better than doing it with teeth.

"Something like that." Dave lifted the freezer lid, showing me hundreds of bags of blood, ready to thaw. Frozen meals.

"Listen." He let the lid close. "I've never been one to pry. I understand our nature—natures—are a bit unorthodox. It's one thing to have an illegal blood bank and use it for nourishment, it's a whole other to collect murderers, turn them into animals and keep them locked up in squalor. But now, I'm—"

"You're wondering if they were blood donors too," I said.

"That's exactly it," he agreed. "You think you can, I don't know, whip up a spell that confirms my theory?"

"I can try."

But no matter what combination of words I used, or how apt the rhyme (Dave helped), nothing happened. No magic of any sort.

Thirty minutes later, we were still exactly where we started.

"Hey, it was worth a try," he said, defeated.

"Maybe Gran can help," I suggested.

"Maybe." His eyes got shifty when he said it, and I wondered if he had an ulterior motive for choosing me. After all, Trish was great at summoning spells—she'd taught me how to perform them.

Or maybe Dave found me as interesting as I found him. Or maybe I was reading too much into things—which is kind of my modus operandi.

When we got into the car, my phone chirped.

"Hmm..."

"What?"

"A new episode of *Creel Creek After Dark,*" I told Dave. "I guess her alibi is ready for ears."

He raised an eyebrow. "If you want to put it on, I'm game."

He offered me a cable to plug my phone into the stereo system.

"You're sure?"

He smiled. "Oh, I'm dying to hear what I've been missing."

23

CREEL CREEK AFTER DARK EPISODE 46

IT'S GETTING LATE.

Very late.
The creeping dread of tomorrow haunts your dreams.
It's dark out. Are you afraid?
Welcome to Creel Creek After Dark.

Athena: I'm your host, Athena Hunter.

Ivana: And I'm the lovely Ivana Steak. Sorry that we're whispering. But as promised, tonight's show is a doozy.

Athena: Or it should be. We're live on location—sitting in the car—at the entrance of Creel Creek's Armand Vineyard.

Ivana: We're waiting for the last employees to leave. Hence the whispering.

Athena: Now, some of you may be wondering what on Earth we're doing at a vineyard because the picture in your mind is a quaint manor on a hillside surrounded by grapevines.

Ivana: Paint the picture for them, Athena.

Athena: Well, it's not anything like Napa Valley, I can tell you that much. There are grapevines—at least I think that's what those are.

Ivana: You mean those things surrounded by an electric fence?

Athena: Yes! It's like they think the grapes might traipse off like cattle. Or, more likely, like they're worried someone might try to steal them. I will say, the main gate is built of some pretty sturdy stuff.

Ivana: It's like we're waiting outside the velociraptor paddock at Jurassic Park.

Athena: And that manor on the hill is—

Ivana: Is straight out of my nightmares.

Athena: Ivana, would you like to do the honors?

Ivana: I think I already did.

Athena: Okay. Why don't you tell our audience some of the vineyard's history?

Ivana: All right, I'll try.

We know the vineyard has been in operation since the mid-1800s. It's family owned, or it has been. That must've ended last month when the owner, Mr. Armand, died. Don't feel too bad— by the look of him he was probably a hundred and ten years old.

Athena: At least a hundred and ten. Okay, I'll take it from here.

What our listeners must be wondering is why a vineyard would be locked up like this. They're used to vineyards that do tours and tastings. Ours doesn't.

Ivana: Not technically true, Athena. They do tastings. Every Wednesday. By invitation only.

Athena: And we don't know anyone who's ever been invited.

Ivana: So, tonight we're inviting ourselves. Everything shuts down around nine o'clock. We've been here since seven and it's nine on the dot. The last employee's car just pulled out.

Ivana: If only some intrepid person knew the gate code.

Athena: Oh, one intrepid person does. She eagle-eyed the employees punching them in from behind those bushes over there.

For the safety of our listeners, I won't be sharing the code.

Ping. Ring. Ping. Ping. OOOOOOOONK!

Ivana: Okay. We're in.

Commercial break: *This episode is brought to you by Armand Wines. Reds. Whites. And blends. All at affordable prices. Find us online or where fine wines are sold.*

Athena: And we're back. We spared you the unremarkable drive up to the house.

Ivana: Cause we're nice like that.

Athena: You're nice. I'm not. I'm snarky.

Ivana: Not that again. Let's sneak inside.

Athena: With our incredible burglary skills, we—

Ivana: The door was unlocked.

Athena: They didn't *have* to know that.

Okay, I'm a little disappointed. There's really not much to it. It looks like a winery. There's a bar and a tasting room. The decorations are interesting. They remind me of—of ancient Egypt with some Paris flair and a little Rome thrown in for good measure. There's also a residence attached. Also unremarkable. The only thing left to do is visit the cellar.

Ivana: The cellar? As in downstairs? As in, the basement?

Athena: I'm sure it's just wine racks, Ivana. She looks as if we might see a ghost, which is probably what our listeners are hoping for. We should give them what they want.

That reminds me. Today's episode is brought to you by Creel Creek Vineyards. Fine wine for people willing to pay.

Ivana: You made that slogan up yourself, didn't you?

Athena: Totally. And they didn't sponsor the show—not yet. If we take a bottle or two, then it's almost like they did, isn't it?

Ivana: I'll drink to that, Athena. Now, let's get this cellar visit over with so I can get some beauty sleep.

Athena: *Creak. Creak. Creak.*

Ivana: Athena! Are you making sound effects?

Athena: Well, the stairs aren't as creaky as I thought they'd be. This Addams Family house is well maintained.

Ivana: Almost like they care about the place and the wine they make here.

Athena: Oh, you think you're cute. Wait... I don't see any wine down here. It's pretty much empty.

Ivana: And dark. Very dark.

Athena: It's empty, and it's dark. The only thing down here is—that's odd.

Ivana: Is that what I—

Athena: More decor. It's like the stuff upstairs. They must've moved it down here for whatever reason. Folks, it's a sarcophagus, if you'll believe it.

Ivana: Fancy. It looks real. Do you think there's a mummy inside it?

Athena: There's only one way to find out.

Ivana: But, should we?

Athena: Listeners want to know. We didn't illegally enter this place and come all the way down here to not peek inside. Now, help me pry it open. I'm setting my phone down. Yes, our state-of-the-art recording system is a phone.

Rustle. Rustle. Creaaaaaak.

Ivana: Oh my God!

Athena: There *is* a mummy inside. It's wrapped up head to toe. But it doesn't look like any mummy I've ever seen. You know, like in the pictures.

Ivana: What she means is it doesn't look fragile. It's not like a skeleton at all. It almost looks like an incredibly detailed Halloween costume. Like it could get up and—

Athena: You saw that, right?

Ivana: Saw what?

Athena: It moved.

Ivana: No, I was just saying—Oh, God. It did move!

Athena: Oh, my—

Rustling sounds.

Footsteps.

Panting.

Engine starting.

Engine sounds.

More panting.

24

IN WITCH I GET FIRED

They ended the episode with a recap. It was like a podcast version of *The Blair Witch Project*. Would an average audience member believe them? Did I believe them? And did they really break into the winery the night of Mr. Caulfield's murder?

A couple of weeks ago, I would never for one second believe the winery would have a mummy in a sarcophagus. Now, my mind was more open. Witches, werewolves, vampires. Why not mummies?

"So," I said.

"So," Dave replied.

I smiled. "They broke into the vineyard. Isn't that a crime?"

"Technically, yes," Dave acknowledged. "But they didn't take anything. The door was open. And Mr. Tadros hasn't pressed charges."

"Does he know they were there?"

Dave raised an eyebrow at me.

"You mean... He's really a mummy, isn't he." It wasn't a question.

"That's my guess," he agreed. "Not that he'll come out and say so. I don't think he's used to all this."

As if on cue, a low and dense fog rolled through the trees and onto the road ahead of us, about a foot high. It was dark, and the waxing moon hung low in the sky.

"Valley fog," I said absentmindedly.

"Valley what?"

"Valley fog." I motioned. "You know—from the mountains."

Dave shook his head. The SUV *swooshed* through the mist. It swirled behind us like stirring cream into tea.

"Your grandmother hasn't taken the time to explain much, has she."

"I haven't taken the time to let her. I've been out of the house every chance I can get."

"As I understand it," he said, "the fog is part of a spell. It's to keep the locals from trying to figure things out. And it works, for the most part."

This lined up with things I'd learned from both Trish and Gran. And it made sense Mr. Caulfield was leery when Hal tried to explain the phenomena to me.

Lucky there was a meteorological explanation for it.

Except—except the spell wasn't working for some reason.

"Jade and Summer," I wondered aloud, "they know something's up. Don't they?"

"It's hard to say," Dave said. "On one hand, this is a show, they're entertaining people. How much they believe is my question. We should be careful. We can't let on that we think it's anything more than entertainment. You understand?"

"I do," I said. "And I really need to get home to Gran and tell her about all of this."

"And I need to pick up my daylight potion."

"And I need to know more about my magic so I can figure out what happened between my mother and the Faction."

Dave's head jerked around so he could gape at me. He pulled it together and went back to watching the road and the growing tendrils of thick fog.

I thought the serious talk must be over. I sort of wanted to go back to the way things were the other day at the park —to Just Dave and Constance.

"Your mother," Dave said slowly. "Did you just say she joined the Faction?"

No such luck.

Like the day slipping to night, the mood in the car darkened. "That's what Gran told me. I don't know much about it. Or her. It happened when I was young."

"Creel Creek is outside of Faction territory," Dave said. "The whole continent is, really. But there're cells in most big cities—New York, Los Angeles, Chicago, New Orleans, and the biggest, in DC. So we're not too far from where they operate."

"What do they do?" I asked.

"A little of everything. Just like politicians, they've got their hands in many pies." He shook his head. "Just like witches."

"It's *only* witches?" I asked. Gran hadn't explained anything. I'd assumed all paranormals were welcome.

"You'll find that most supernatural beings like to stick with their own kind. The Faction is made up of witches and warlocks."

"Warlocks? Really?"

"Yeah."

Trish had put the idea in my head that warlocks were

like the Slytherins of the Harry Potter Universe. Mostly bad apples, and always looking for the catch.

But Gran had said the Faction wasn't all bad. These opinions were contradictory.

"What do *you* think? Good guys or bad guys?"

"It depends on your point of view," he said.

"Pretend you're me. My point of view."

"I think you need to make up your own mind," he said.

"Bad then. At least that's the vibe I keep getting."

He smiled. I could see the white of his teeth.

"When this blows over," I said, not meaning the fog, "the murder case, I mean. Do you think maybe you can help me find out more about my mom?"

"You want me to help you find dirt on the Faction?"

"I guess so."

Dave pulled into Gran's drive. "It sounds not very smart," he said. "Then again, I've never been good at saying no to a pretty girl."

He thinks I'm pretty?

My hair was a mess. I felt grimy. And I didn't put on any makeup this morning.

"So, yes, then?" I asked.

"Probably," he answered. "You be careful at work around Jade, all right? Actually, just be careful in general. There really might be a hunter."

"You do the same, Sheriff."

For a second, in that SUV in front of Gran's house, it felt like the end of a long date. I wanted to kiss him, to feel his prickly stubble on my cheek. I wanted to know how soft his lips were.

But then a raccoon clambered up and perched on the porch railing, ruining the moment.

I KNEW I'd be walking on eggshells around Jade. I just wasn't expecting them to crack so soon.

The next morning, she called me into her office as soon as I set foot in the store. She wasn't going to give me a pass, not after an attempted robbery at my register—or the police interview and its aftermath.

"I haven't clocked in," I told her.

"There'll be no need for that," she retorted ominously.

Eggshells be damned. I was going to crack them. "What? You're firing me?"

"That's about the gist of it." Jade steepled her hands atop Mr. Caulfield's desk. She looked as cool as a cucumber, as comfortable as one could be in a vampire's chair.

"But... but, why? I'm a good worker. I'm punctual. I've memorized half of the produce chart. Is this about yesterday?"

"It's not about the robbery," Jade said. "And you're not punctual, whatever you believe."

I was five minutes early. Aside from the day I was stopped for speeding, I'd never been late.

"Are you serious? Did someone tell you that Cyrus offered me this job?"

Jade's glare was as sharp as she probably kept her knives.

"Don't play innocent," she sneered. "It's not a good look on you. I told you on day one I had a hunch about you. I know the sheriff was at your grandmother's house a few days after the murder. I know he stopped you the day before."

"For speeding."

She wasn't having it. "You must have a record for him to

get involved so quickly. Then whatever happened yesterday —another death? I know you were there."

"To help."

"There's something off about you, Constance. You've heard our show. You know we get to the bottom of everything. I wish you'd just tell me what's going on."

I really didn't need this. At that point, I was happy to be fired and get out of there. But I couldn't leave without having my say.

Jade was ready. "I was suspicious of you the day you started," she said. "And I did some digging. You know what I found?"

She was waiting for me, so I said, "Obviously I don't."

"You had a traumatic childhood."

This was getting silly. "Oh, that's your evidence, is it?"

Enough was enough. I turned to leave.

"Tell me, what did Eric do to you to deserve such a gruesome fate?"

She did not just say that.

My fingers began to burn, a lot like the sensation after touching a hot pan. "I didn't kill Mr. Caulfield. I didn't even know him—not like you and your friend Summer."

On the podcast, she'd intimated he was the Creel Creek Bloodsucker.

"You knew him well," I said. "And you're obviously hiding something. Give it up. Or just shut up."

Something fiery leaped from my fingertips in Jade's direction.

Did I just cast a spell? By rhyming up with up? I grimaced —I always hated when songwriters did that.

But where had the spell gone? There was no fire that I could see. But the coffee pot behind Jade was glowing. And her face was blank, expressionless.

"Blood," she said.

"What about it?"

"Blood," she said again.

"What about blood?" I clenched my fist. "Dammit, this is getting old."

She shook her head, a little dazed. "You're still here?"

"I never left," I told her. "What were you just saying about blood?"

She shook her head forcefully, like she was pushing something to the back of her mind. "I was saying that you're fired, Constance. We'll mail your last check. Now, leave. Don't force me to call your friend, the sheriff. I doubt he wants to see you so soon after your last visit."

25

IN WITCH I WAIT THREE DAYS FOR A PHONE CALL...

And maybe Jade was right. Because Dave didn't want to see me after our last visit. A few days went by without him so much as calling or texting.

Isn't that what friends do?

I thought—I hoped—we were friends. Maybe I'd been mistaken about the nature of our relationship.

Then again, he did have his plate full. Three girls. A murder to solve. Maybe two. And I realized that there was also a full moon to contend with.

So, I cut him some slack.

At least I had one real friend in Trish. With so much going on at the grocery store, she needed help at the bookstore and was kind enough to offer employment. It wasn't much. Few hours, less money, and a lot less to do.

She showed me the system for orders that came from the online store, then how to package and ready them for the post office.

She told me not to worry about anything else, insisting I wasn't to waste my time cleaning, despite the cobwebs in every dusty corner. The floors needed an industrial pressure washer.

I searched for a broom anyway, but I didn't find anything conventional. Tucked in a corner, I found an old ornamental broom, twisted and forgotten. If this was Harry Potter, it'd be one of the old school brooms, not a sleek and aerodynamic state-of-the-art broom like the Firebolt.

I wasn't going to try to sweep with it, but I did ask Trish about it—like was it used to fly.

"I guess it might do in a pinch," she said coyly.

"Have you flown before?"

"Constance, someone in town would notice."

"I thought everyone in town was under some sort of spell or something."

"Not a spell. Not exactly. It's just, there's history in the earth. They grow up aware something is off about Creel Creek, but they don't know what."

"Oh." Not exactly how Dave had put it.

"As long as we're careful, they won't be any the wiser. But I think they might notice a witch flying a broomstick."

"I think Jade and Summer have noticed a lot."

"Yes, well, with the solstice coming, we should be extra careful."

"What happens on the solstice?"

"Equinoxes, solstices, and cross-quarter days are when shifts occur. Shifts in perspective. On Halloween—a cross-quarter day, by the way—it's a little worse. That's the one day of the year when our true forms show. It's not just in Creel Creek, either. You can go anywhere, and people will see you for what you are. Hence it was declared a day for everyone to dress up. When everyone is pretending, we don't have to." She smiled.

"Okay." That was a problem for another time. But the

solstice was approaching fast. There were flyers up advertising the Midsummer Festival, the one Dave's little girl had told me about. They'd already started to decorate Main Street.

I watched them from the store. Stuck there with nothing to do but read or listen to Jade's podcast, I listened to every episode, hoping for more information about the town and its strange inhabitants. But most of the tidbits were about Jade and Summer—or rather, their alter egos.

I went back to books.

Weird, I'd dreamed for so long magic was real. I thought I'd be a Hermione when I was really a Harry or Ron. Spell books weren't my jam. Fiction was.

I combed the shelves, looking for a mystery that suited my taste—which of course brought my mind back to the murder. If it wasn't me, and it wasn't Jade or Summer, then who was it?

Cyrus Tadros had an alibi. When Mr. Caulfield was killed, he was wrapped up in bandages.

I couldn't shake the feeling that something else was going on there, some other lie, something I couldn't put my finger on. *And speaking of fingers*, I thought, *what did they do in Jade's office?*

I stared down at my hands like they were going to tell me.

The door chimed. Maybe it was Dave with news or just wanting to talk. I'd take anyone to talk to. Sometimes, Twinkie peeked from her hiding place at the register. She and Brad frequently went off to the shadow realm to do whatever familiars do there. Today, she was asleep and Brad was nowhere to be found.

And aside from a few online orders, I hadn't had any

customers for days. As far as I knew, the last person to enter the shop was Cyrus.

It was neither Cyrus nor Dave. It was a hook nosed, redheaded reporter.

With the words *hidden agenda* practically written on her forehead, Summer Shields simpered in my direction. She took the first left and went down the romance aisle, pretending to browse. Like everything else in the store not having to do with magic, those shelves were filled with old mass market paperbacks with yellowed pages. She picked one at random, then strode toward the counter, her eyes locked on mine with the sort of confidence required of a TV personality.

My fingertips tingled. It was my fight-or-flight response reminding me that magic coursed through my veins. I could use it at will.

"We looked you up," she said, slamming her book down next to the register.

"So I heard."

It seemed I had brought down the wrath of both women.

"You have quite a history," she said. "Lost your mom at the age you needed her the most, got married in Vegas, then there must've been a dozen articles about the little startup you worked for. I found your divorce petition too. It seems you're still married. Does your boyfriend know?"

"My boyfriend?"

"The sheriff."

"I wouldn't call him that."

He hasn't called.

I wasn't going to let her get to me. If she was just here to be petty, then why waste anything—my magic or my time. Summer Shields wasn't worth it.

"Will this be it?" I asked her, flipping the book over.

Mass market books were seventy-five percent off their cover price. This one had a cheap imitation Fabio on the cover, not the real thing.

"You probably think you're hot stuff, don't you," Summer sneered. "A hotshot city girl from California, moving here to the sticks. If you plan on outing us, well, I'll beat you to it. I'll announce it on the next episode. I don't care."

"What are you even talking about?" I had no plans to out anyone.

"I'm talking about the podcast," she spat. "I know that you know—I mean that you know it's me and Jade."

"So? It's just a podcast."

"It's not a joke, even if everyone thinks it is."

I knew it wasn't, but I couldn't tell her.

"We're going to expose Creel Creek for what it really is," Summer said. "That's always been the plan. We expose this place, we introduce ourselves to the world. Then we monetize. Books and merchandise. Maybe even a TV show—I have the connections."

If that's the case, I wondered, *then why aren't you already on the Discovery channel?*

"Just what is it you think Creel Creek is, exactly?" I asked her.

Summer wanted to expose Creel Creek for the payoff. Investigative journalism, the podcast, and even the paranormal town she lived in were just a means to an end. She didn't care about any of them.

"I think it's..." The snarl in her voice unsnarled. The sneer on her face unsneered. She glanced over her shoulder, then whispered. "I think it's haunted."

I rolled my eyes, and her momentary honesty was gone. "You're just like everyone else. This town is tricking you. You can't see what's really going on."

"And what's really going on, Summer?"

She squeaked and grabbed my arm as I jumped, both of us startled by someone else in the store.

Cyrus Tadros had evaded the chime on the front door.

"Cyrus!" Summer clutched her chest, relieved.

Normally, I'd be doing the same. But in my surprise, I'd sent a spark flying. My magic had taken over my instincts.

I checked for damage and found Twinkie glaring from her hiding spot in the drawer under the register. A little singed, the rodent folded her tiny arms.

"Sorry," I mouthed.

"There's nothing to be sorry about," Cyrus said. "You two were arguing, and I thought it best not to interrupt."

More like he wanted to eavesdrop.

Summer was more taken with his charm than I was. "Cyrus," she said again, "what brings you here?"

She said it with disbelief, like no one *actually* shopped here—not even her. The romance novel was sure to be left behind as she inched closer to the too-handsome man.

He had a bottle of wine in one hand and a book in the other. "I'm returning a book," he said. "For store credit, of course. Maybe someone else will find it useful. And I brought a bottle of wine as an apology. I heard about what happened the other day at the grocery store."

He tucked the book under his arm so Summer couldn't read the cover. If she did, she'd probably be thrilled that someone else shared her suspicions about Creel Creek.

She had to see that he was a major player. After all, it was his vineyard with a mummy in the cellar.

"Are you still going on about this stuff?" he asked her. "The strange happenings of Creel Creek?" He graced her with a smile.

His charm was apparently overwhelming. "You're right," she said. "It's silly."

"Although I'm sure the little joke I played didn't fool you for a second." Cyrus turned to me. "It sounded plausible, yes? The key was not letting either of them in on it—until after, of course."

Summer nodded earnestly.

"It's not that I didn't trust your acting ability," Cyrus said, pouring it on, "but Jade, she's more local theater to your Hollywood."

Now I was lost.

Cyrus turned to me. "I had to fool them, you see."

"We were fooled," Summer agreed meekly. "I really thought the vineyard was haunted. I thought I'd seen a mummy. That is, until Cyrus came forward the next day and offered a sponsorship. He explained how he'd been listening to the show—he knew we'd surely investigate. He caught me on camera that morning when I got the gate code. He staged that too. You know the rest."

"It was a little fun," Cyrus teased. "And great marketing on my part. Sales are up forty percent this week."

"I'm glad," Summer said, not looking it. Every ounce of steam she'd stormed in here with had vanished. All that remained was Summer Shields, ordinary Creel Creek citizen.

"We'll have to do it again sometime. I'm sure next week's episode is a doozy."

"It is," Summer replied. "It was good seeing you, Cyrus."

And just like I said she would, she left without imitation Fabio. I set the book and its man-chest aside and took the one from Cyrus.

"You're such a liar." The words escaped my mouth as soon as I'd thought them.

He chuckled. "The customer service here never disappoints. Is there a card I can fill out?" He pretended to look for one. "This is twice now that I've been greeted with churlishness. You should be more appreciative of my patronage."

"You're returning a book. That's not patronage."

"I brought wine."

"You lied to her," I said. "You really are a mummy."

"I'm not *just* a mummy," he boasted. "And I don't remember you telling her about being a witch. I bet you could get your own episode."

"Well," I countered, "she didn't interrupt *my* potion-making. Did you really know they were lurking around? How did this sponsorship happen?"

"I'll tell you over dinner."

"You'll what?"

"Oh." He shrugged nonchalantly. "It seemed as good a time as any to ask you out."

"I'm serious," I said. "Did you know they were going to be there? I don't think you did. You just got lucky playing it off. You heard what she's trying to do. She's dangerous."

"She's a fly that needs swatting. This is my best wine, by the way. Vintage."

"Tell me," I pleaded, "are you really a mummy?"

"I'll tell you anything you want to know over dinner. What do you say?"

"Tell me now."

"Agree to dinner, and I will."

"Okay. Fine."

"Okay." He looked smug. "I'll tell you over dinner. Friday night. At the vineyard. The gate will be open."

"I didn't agree to have dinner *alone* with you," I protested. "And you said you'd tell me now."

"No, I said I'd tell you anything you wanted. Not when.

And we won't be dining alone. My staff will be there. Is that good enough?"

"Not really," I said.

"But you'll come anyway?"

I shrugged.

"I'll see you Friday," he said.

"Friday." What else could I say? I wanted answers. And he was going to give them to me.

26

LIAR, LIAR

Friday night came far too quickly.

Unsurprisingly, both Gran and Trish tried to talk me out of going. Even Brad was concerned.

"I know I'm new at this," he boomed. "But protecting you from the undead could prove difficult. You hardly know any spells. You're not quick on your feet. And you aren't bringing backup."

"I didn't know mummies existed." Stevie leaped up on my bed and curled next to the raccoon. "Not that I'm an expert."

They stayed while I dressed, offering commentary on my attire. While concerned for my safety, their host bodies' tendencies won out. By the time I was ready, they were asleep.

"I thought you said this was a date." Stevie cracked an eye open.

"I said I didn't want it to be a date. Just dinner."

"Dinner with a handsome undead fellow."

"Something like that."

I went to the bathroom to, as Gran would say, put on my

face. When I returned, Stevie remarked, "I thought you said this wasn't a date."

"I can still look nice!"

I stuck my tongue out at the cat and hurried down the stairs, leaving the familiars on the bed. No backup. I couldn't really take Brad with me anywhere. He'd have to use his otherworldly senses to keep me out of harm's way.

Gran was the prying type. She gave me a speculative eye from her recliner in the den. "I think you might be sending mixed signals. Jeans, really? On a date?"

"It's not a date! And they're comfortable."

"How much eyeliner does it take to walk the streets these days?" she said about my miserable attempt at wings.

"It's the style," I told her. "All the girls are doing it."

"That's right. *Girls*. A woman of forty should know how to dress for a date."

"For the last time, it's not a date," I huffed. "It's dinner. It's me digging for information."

"For the last time," Gran retorted, "it's not your job to sleuth. If it's about the vampire murder, then shouldn't the sheriff be involved?"

"It's not about the vampire murder," I lied.

A white lie. Mr. Caulfield's death *was* on my mind, but there was a lot we didn't know about Cyrus Tadros—about the undead. About mummies.

"I think you should let the sheriff know what you're up to," Gran told me. "When was the last time you spoke with him?"

"Before I got fired," I replied.

"You're blaming him, aren't you?"

"Not exactly."

Yes, I did. He'd played a part in my termination, but not deliberately. I was angrier that he hadn't called. I was hoping for an apology. Had *he* offered me dinner, I wouldn't be wearing jeans right now.

Crookshanks purred to life and I drove through town. Main Street was ready for the Midsummer Festival. White lights twinkled up and down the thoroughfare.

I drove past the track to Nell's cabin. I would have missed it but they left a cone to mark it.

The vineyard was a further fifteen miles out of town. It was creepy, more *Addams Family* than *The Munsters*—there is a difference!

The gate was open. I eased Crookshanks around a circular drive, parking next to a fountain with no water.

Like Cyrus had promised, a member of his staff was there to greet me.

Adding to the experience, his butler exuded Addams Family vibes. Uncle Fester vibes. He had a gleaming bald head and heavy bags under his eyes. To top it off, he wore a name tag proclaiming him to be Lurque.

"How is that pronounced?" I asked him.

"Lurk," he said. "It's French. This way, Madame."

"It's, uh, Mademoiselle actually."

Lurque smirked. I'm sorry, that's what he did. "Whatever you say, Madame. We actually did away with the use of Mademoiselle a few years ago."

He led me to a large dining room with three long tables in the center. Only one was set for dinner. Dinner for two. A sideboard was prepped with a pitcher of water and opened bottles of wine.

Lurque seated me, comedically at the end of the long table. It reminded me of the scene when Bruce Wayne and Vicki Vale have dinner in the first *Batman* movie. I was going to have to shout for Cyrus to hear me.

"Monsieur Tadros will be joining you shortly. He's tied up at the moment."

"Thank you," I said, my confidence growing. On dates, I'm typically clumsy.

Th*is isn't a date,* I reminded myself.

Lurque departed and another member of staff filled my wine while yet another served soup. She put bread in the center of the table, well out of my reach.

The way the eccentric undead man had strongarmed me into this evening, this quasi-date, I didn't imagine he'd allow me to go much longer without his presence.

The servants left me, alone in the room. They returned twenty minutes later, scooping up my untouched soup and replacing it with salad. I was happy for a fresh glass of wine —that had been touched. Except I remembered a little too late that alcohol had no effect on me thanks to Hilda's gift.

"Is this a game?" I asked, not having any fun.

"Monsieur Tadros will join you shortly, Madame."

"When?"

"Monsieur Tadros prefers to dine in the kitchen but will take his coffee and dessert here with you."

"Surely you're joking."

Irritation crossed over the possibly French, maybe Italian, servant. "Surely, I am not."

"Then, can I dine in the kitchen?"

"Monsieur Tadros prefers his guests to dine in the dining room. He prefers that no one watch him eat."

"Does he eat?"

She chose not to answer.

If only Gran could see what kind of date this was turning out to be. Thankfully, the jeans were comfy.

I took the salad and my wine, scooted my chair back, and made for the swinging doors after Miss Possibly French.

If I wanted to eat alone, I could've stayed at Gran's—I could've eaten at the bar at Orange Blossom's. Neither would have stuck me in a room by myself.

"You've got a lot of nerve," I said, catching sight of him.

Still on his salad course, he covered his mouth with a hand. "Constance," he said, "give me one second to finish chewing."

"One," I said, like a child.

He laughed, and I noticed a bowl sitting next to him.

"Allow me another." He turned away from me, taking the bowl, and when he was done chewing, he spit the food into it. "I'm missing a few vital organs needed for things like digestion."

I didn't know what to say, but my gag reflex was going off the charts.

"Let me explain. My restorative process, well, it doesn't work on everything. I'm still very much what you'd imagine on the inside."

"You really are a mummy," I said, not as shocked as I sounded.

"Not a mummy. I'm *the* mummy," he said again, like that should mean something.

"I'm Osiris. Perhaps you've heard of me? God of the undead, among other things. When my brother Set cut me into pieces, my wife, Isis, who was a witch like you, wrapped my body with a restorative dressing. I returned to life not only healed but with a youthful vigor."

"You're married?"

"I *was* married. So were you, as I understand it."

This again.

I did some mental calculations.

"That's what you were doing the night of the podcast. You were here restoring yourself. And you scared them away." Then I understood. "Your father never died, did he? You're Mr. Armand. You and he are the same person. Mummy. Whatever."

"I wasn't going to explain that, if I could help it." Cyrus smiled. "Then again, I guess I didn't have to."

"You're a liar."

"No, no. The part about living in Europe is true, although it was four centuries ago. And it wasn't with my mother."

"You dog."

"What can I say?" He shrugged. "I've lived a long and full life. Many lives. And just so you know, when I visited the bookshop, I did need the book. That wasn't a lie. Something is amiss."

"And that is?"

"This house used to be haunted. I'm serious. There were ghosts residing here, many from around the time of the civil war. One day, they just vanished without a trace. Then a vampire died."

"And a witch."

"Which witch?" Cyrus narrowed his eyes.

"Her name was Nell Baker," I told him. "She lived on this side of town."

"Yes," Cyrus said with contempt, "I'm familiar with Nell. A bit of a nuisance. Always had her hand in several cauldrons, if you know what I mean."

There was something bothering me, something niggling the back of my mind. But I couldn't figure out what it had to do with Cyrus.

A chef appeared and asked, "Are you ready for the main course, sir?" His Southern drawl stood out.

Cyrus looked at me. "What do you say? Is it all right if I join you?"

My stomach grumbled. *Traitor.* "Sounds good."

Cyrus returned with me to the dining room and took a seat close to mine, not the one set at the other end of the table. He sipped wine while I ate steak, Brussels sprouts, and mashed potatoes. There was coffee and dessert wine to pair with a red velvet cake, which was moist and perfect.

I relented, listening to stories from his youth in Egypt and his travels across the world. We chatted about the vineyard and Creel Creek's own history. Then I asked why he'd come here when he could be anywhere he wanted.

"I moved here to be with someone," he said sadly. "We had heard about a place accepting of our kind."

I didn't know exactly what—or who—he meant. I was about to press further when Lurque interrupted our conversation.

"There's someone at the door," he told my host.

"Did you tell them to bugger off?"

"I did, sir. But they're quite insistent they must speak with you. I'm afraid they didn't give me any choice in the matter."

"What do you mean?" Cyrus asked with a scowl.

Lurque stepped away from the doorframe, then Willow and Dave appeared. Dave, with his gun drawn. Willow was holding handcuffs.

"Constance?"

"Dave?"

The sheriff shook his head grimly.

"Cyrus Tadros, Edward Armand, whoever the hell you *really* are," he said, "you're under arrest for the murder of Eric Caulfield."

"Arrest?"

"He couldn't have done it," I protested. "He was on that podcast too. You heard it."

"The thing about poisoning," Dave said as Willow slapped the cuffs on Cyrus, "is the poisoner doesn't have to be there when it happens."

I finally connected the dots. I remembered by Cyrus's own admission Mr. Armand and Mr. Caulfield hadn't gotten along.

I wondered if that was always the case or if it was a recent development. His last words really struck me. He'd moved here for someone.

I could only guess who that someone was.

27

IN WITCH SOMEONE'S PANTS ARE ON FIRE

I thought for sure Dave would question me at the vineyard and let me go on to Gran's on my own, no big deal.

Wrong.

Dave hardly spoke to me. But lately, that was par for the course. He hadn't spoken to me in days. Not that I'd tried to contact him. But still, it irked me.

At least he allowed me to sit in the front of his car when they drove us in for questioning. Questioning—like I had some connection to this, aside from being in the wrong place at the wrong time.

If anything, that was what I seemed to have a knack for —I was a wrong place, wrong time kind of gal.

Three times during the drive, it looked as if Dave was going to say something. Each time, he stopped himself and sighed, irritated.

It was like he was personally affronted I was there.

I asked him a dozen questions, but only in my head. My mind was doing somersaults trying to figure out the clues he'd put together without me. The connection between Cyrus and Mr. Caulfield.

I guessed it was some sort of lovers' quarrel between beings that had loved and lived with each other for centuries. Who knew how long they'd been apart—or how long they'd been together?

Cyrus had basically told me as much. He must've moved to Creel Creek to be with Mr. Caulfield.

Then something happened. Things went sour. And Cyrus acted. It was a perfect way to get away with murder—using his magical wrappings to turn old Edward Armand into the young and debonair Cyrus Tadros.

How did Dave figure it out?

I bit my lip, anxious to ask him.

But Dave left me in an interrogation room. It was just like the ones on TV, with the two-way mirror and everything. Although I suspected no one was on the other side.

I assumed Dave was going to talk to Cyrus first. Get his side of things.

Time did one of those things where ten minutes felt like ten hours. I was tired and full from the delicious dinner Cyrus's chef had served. I'd almost nodded off, slumped in my chair, when Dave opened the door.

He looked tired. Pale. A little thinner than I remembered.

"Well, he's not talking," Dave said, closing the door and taking the seat opposite me. "He lawyered up. And his power-broker DC attorney can't drive down here until next week."

Still feeling sluggish and sleepy, I didn't know what he wanted me to say. Was I back on the case after the silent car ride?

I was about to lay into him, but he stopped me before I could speak.

"Can you just—" He shook his head, obviously fighting back anger. "Can you just tell me what exactly you were thinking? What were you doing there?"

He sounded almost like he was jealous. *Almost*. I put that thought away for safekeeping.

"I was having dinner," I said. "He asked me out. That's not allowed?"

"It's allowed." He wouldn't look at me. "But you had to know that man was on my radar for the murder."

"No," I exclaimed. "How would I know that? You never told me. Heck, you haven't talked to me since you asked for my help the other day. You know I got fired for that, right?"

"I—No, I didn't. It's been a weird couple of days. I'm sorry about that."

He finally met my eyes. "This is going to come out of left field, I know, but I was trying to protect you. I like you, Constance. I haven't liked anyone, not like this, in a long time. I thought I—"

"You like me?" My traitorous heart fluttered. *Remember —we're mad at him...*

"I did." He flushed. "Or I do. I do." He huffed. "Don't get me off track, Constance. Tell me what you were *really* doing there. And does it have any connection to the case? I need complete honesty."

"Kind of." He wanted the truth, so I was going to give it to him. "I was trying to help—trying to get some information about Cyrus. I mean, he asked me to dinner. I took him up on it to get the scoop about the whole mummy thing. I didn't think he was the murderer or anything. You remember the podcast. I was just interested."

We discussed Cyrus's past, trading information we'd

gathered. Me, over the course of dinner, and Dave over the last few days.

The theory I came up with on the silent ride was correct. Cyrus and Mr. Caulfield had a long connection with each other. And like the Cullens from *Twilight*, they'd been calling Creel Creek home since the town's founding in the 18th century.

They were both ancient beings. Cyrus had as many centuries as most humans get in years.

"That's a lot of time to learn about vampires," I said. "And their weaknesses."

"That it is," Dave agreed. "There's just one thing that's bothering me."

"That is?" I asked, not sharing his concern.

"I don't have proof." He struggled for a moment before deciding to let me in. "See, Mr. Caulfield drank coffee every morning. Had his own coffeemaker in his office. And from what we've gathered, he mixed a packet of blood with it."

He'd mentioned something like this before at Gran's house. Still, I gagged at the thought of sullying coffee that way.

"So, he takes a blood from his freezer every morning. Drops it in the coffee. For all we know, that tainted packet could've been there quite some time before he picked it up. But I don't think so. The timing seems too perfect to be a coincidence—right when Cyrus was making his transition. They had to know each other's habits."

"Maybe. Or maybe he didn't do it."

Dave looked at me skeptically. I couldn't blame him, after the evidence he'd laid out. However speculative it was, it did seem like he was on the right track. Except my instincts told me to look elsewhere.

"Do I really need to ask you to elaborate?"

"No," I said, still racking my brain for what my intuition, or my witchy instincts, were trying to tell me. "I was so mad. I forgot about something Jade said to me when I was fired."

Dave looked interested.

"She said something about blood."

"What about blood?"

"Nothing, really. She shut down after she said it. It was almost like that possum guy in the woods. Maybe she knows something. Or she knew about the blood and told someone else."

"Maybe," Dave said, then he perked up. "Do you have anywhere you need to be tonight?"

"Besides bed?"

He smiled. "So, no?"

I nodded, but I didn't know where he was going with this. "I'm going to give Jade a call and have her come in. She'll put up a fight, but we'll get her down here tonight and have it out. I'd like you to sit in. When is the witching hour? Midnight?"

I nodded.

Dave gestured at the two-way mirror. "Maybe your magic can be of some assistance. I'd like to try and unlock her secrets. That podcast of hers has me anxious. I think you're right—she does know something. What do you say?"

There was no way I'd say no. I was as curious as anyone to find out what Jade knew about Mr. Caulfield and blood. I only hoped I could help, either make a case against Cyrus, or against whoever the real killer was if it wasn't him. In my mind it wasn't.

It took Jade the better part of an hour to arrive. I sipped tea, not coffee, and sat on the other side of the glass watching her fidget uncomfortably. This was probably what it felt like before she'd fired me. But I was taking no pleasure from it. I felt bad for her.

"I've been listening to your podcast," Dave started.

Jade brightened, then her face went white, and she sunk lower into her seat.

"You didn't listen to episode eight, did you?" she asked nervously.

On my phone, I looked up the details. *Werewolves.*

"I think I missed that one," Dave replied. "Want to give me a recap?"

"No."

"Too bad." He smiled, probably because he had a good idea what it was about. "Can I ask you a question?"

"Isn't that why I'm here?" she said sarcastically. "To answer your questions?"

"Fair enough," he said. "I'm wondering if your show is real or faked."

"You know it's not real," she lied, trying and failing to hide a smile.

"Yes, I know it's not real," Dave said. "But what about you—do you believe it? I'm just asking."

Jade shrugged. "I believe there's some truth in most stories. Fairytale or not."

"And Summer?" Dave asked.

"She believes it."

Dave nodded. "Are the episodes her ideas or yours? What's your input?"

"I hardly see how this has anything to do with—"

"I'm just curious."

"They started out with her ideas," Jade said.

"And now?"

"Well, we've been getting these letters. Anonymous tips.

Stories too. It's how we knew to go to the vineyard that night when, uh, that guy Cyrus played that joke on us."

"I'm guessing you already know he's in lockup."

Jade nodded. "Summer told me. She has a police scanner."

"I'm going to need to see those letters," Dave told her. "My guess is, Mr. Tadros in there started this elaborate hoax to boost his business—and possibly to give him an alibi for the murder."

He looked at the mirror, then at Jade. I wasn't sure if that was my cue or not.

"Can you tell me what you know about blood?"

"What blood?"

"I know you know something about the blood." He looked at the mirror again. It was my cue. "It'd be easier if you just told me. On the podcast, you're the one who knew about the Bloodsucker—as you referred to Eric Caulfield."

"I don't know anything about blood," Jade said. To me, she looked truthful. "It was a joke. He had pale skin, hardly slept, and never wanted to touch garlic."

I didn't think there was anything I could do to force Jade into telling us more than she wanted to.

She'd said blood when we were in her office. And that's when my fingers got hot. I tried to will them to do it now.

Be magical.

"You're sure you don't know anything about blood?"

"I know *nothing* about blood," she insisted.

But that wasn't true. I looked at my hands.

"Tell us what you know," I said under my breath. "Crap, my fingers are starting to glow."

It was a terrible rhyme. Not meant to be a spell.

Two things happened at once. My pants, where my fingertips were, started to smoke. And Jade's face went slack.

She started to talk. I tried to listen, but I had to put my jeans out.

"I was a medic in the Army." Jade spoke in monotone. "Five years ago. Another lifetime. I told Mr. Caulfield about it."

"Jade?" Dave snapped his fingers in front of her face. She continued her story, oblivious.

"One day he asked for my help. There's a blood bank in his basement. I took blood from anyone strapped to the gurney down there. They were never awake. No one else was home. Mr. Caulfield used to laugh and say it was our little secret. Then he'd snap his fingers three times."

Right at the tip of her nose, Dave snapped his fingers three times. Jade came out of her trance, just as she must have when Mr. Caulfield was done with her. He'd used her.

That's what he'd wanted her for that night—only he didn't have enough time to put her in a trance.

"Thanks," Dave said.

"Thanks for what?"

"For your time tonight. I'll let you get back home."

He ushered her out and returned a few minutes later, leaning in the doorway. I could tell his thoughts were a million miles away.

"So, Nell drops the animals off at his place. Jade takes blood. Pretty good system."

"Why not do it himself though? Why risk it?"

"You have instincts, right?"

"Obviously."

"No, I mean being a witch. I'm guessing that was you who put her into that state."

"A happy accident." I indicated my pants. My thighs were showing though several burn holes close to the pockets.

"What I'm trying to say is if his vampire instincts were anything like mine are when I'm a wolf... well, let's just say that being cooped up in tight quarters with blood being drained—I can't imagine it's easy."

"Oh." I couldn't picture Dave as a wolf.

"I've got a lot of work ahead of me tonight." Dave showed me out.

I wasn't in trouble with him anymore. He'd managed to weasel out of trouble with me too.

"Would you mind doing me a favor?" he asked.

"Anything," I said without thinking.

He smiled the thick-mustached smile I'd grown accustomed to. "Well, I was going to ask you not to butt in anymore—and to get better control of your magic. Then you said anything, and well, that gives me an idea."

"Yeah?"

"You know Midsummer Festival is tomorrow night. Technically, I have to work it. But the girls really seemed to like you. Serious, they've talked about you. Would you mind watching them for me?"

"Like babysitting?" This was not where I'd hoped the conversation was going.

"Kind of." He looked embarrassed. "I was thinking more like a date. Except I'll be in my uniform, which some girls kind of like, by the way."

"Some girls," I said.

"I'll have to work if the crowd gets unruly."

"Does it ever get unruly?"

"Never in the thirty-odd years I've been going has it ever gotten unruly."

"It sounds like a date," I said.

And that was exactly how I planned on treating it.

28

THE MIDSUMMER FESTIVAL

Outside, the air was a touch cooler even though it was officially summer. The humidity was high. Clouds had moved in, threatening to rain out the event.

I'd never seen anything quite like the setup on Main Street. The normally deserted street was filled with people and lit with Edison-style lights crisscrossing over the street.

Tiny booths lined each sidewalk from the courthouse down to Bewitched Books and beyond. There was a different carnival game in each. In the street, bounce houses and inflatable slides were crawling with kids.

Dave bought each of his girls big strings of tickets, and we strolled down the street, the girls partaking in anything and everything.

For a while, Kacie didn't want to come out of a bounce house. Then Elsie said she was hungry, which meant she wanted to eat candy. All three wanted popcorn. Dave bought us a funnel cake to share.

"There's only a few nights a year this place seems like a

nice place to live," he said to me. "This is one of 'em, don't you agree?"

"It's nice." I nodded. "But Gran and Trish didn't seem to think so. I invited both of them to come out."

"On *our* date?" he asked, abashed.

"On our babysitting date," I teased him. "I thought they could use the fresh air. Especially Gran."

"And here I was going to say especially Trish." He laughed. "I'm glad you two are getting on so well. It's never fun being the new person in town."

"Oh, so you know my pain, do you?"

He didn't seem like the type of person who ever left town. If he had, it wasn't for long.

"I don't." He shook his head. "But when I was a kid, I always thought it'd be cool to be an Army brat. See the world. It feels like I've been stuck here my whole life."

"If you don't like it, why do you still live here?"

His mouth twitched at the edge of his mustache. "The same reason people everywhere stay put. It's where I grew up. It's where my sister lives. It's where our parents grew up. Where I met my wife and where she grew up."

"Right," I said, unable to come up with anything to follow that.

I followed Dave and the girls up and down the street until their bellies were full of candy and their legs were tired and aching. Kacie asked me to pick her up. Dave carried Elsie on his shoulders.

"There's someone I'd like you to meet," Dave said, motioning up the street. "That pesky sister I was talking about."

A dark-eyed brunette woman struggling to keep up with two boys gave me a look, then she gave Dave one, her eyebrows dancing suggestively.

What is it with this family and their facial expressions? I wondered.

"Is this Constance?" she asked him.

"In the flesh," Dave said. "And Constance, this is my sister, Imogene, and her two boys, Batman and Superman."

"That's not our names, Uncle Dave."

"Oh, sorry." He smiled. "I meant Shaggy and Scooby."

"Wrong again," the other boy said.

"This is Ron and Neville," Imogene corrected. And it wasn't a joke.

Another Potterhead.

"Can we go home?" Allie asked her dad.

Dave checked his watch. "There's still an hour and a half left. We didn't pace ourselves, did we, girls?"

"I can take them," Imogene offered. "We were just headed to the van."

"You sure you don't mind?"

"Not at all." Imogene winked. "It'll give you two some time alone."

"Gross," one of the boys—Neville, I thought—said. Imogene stepped on his toe.

"You're sure you don't mind?" Dave asked her again. "It's not one of your nights."

"Go," she said. "Before I change my mind."

Imogene took the tired Kacie from me while Dave let Elsie down from his shoulders. She was less tired now, eager to play with her two cousins.

"Imogene takes care of the girls on the nights, and the days, I'm at work. She's a great big sister."

"Oh," I said, a bit surprised, "you're the little brother?"

"Is that bad?"

"Aren't little brothers always spoiled?" I asked him.

"Oh, I think I'd be spoiled regardless. I know I have been

—spoiled in life and love. I mean, just look at those girls of mine. I hit the jackpot."

We saw them off, then strolled the midway again. Dave kept one eye out for trouble. But like he said before, there wasn't much going on. The crowd thinned out when most of the children went home to bed.

If one eye was on the crowd, the other was free. I caught it staring down at my hand. The hand I didn't slide into my pocket—just in case.

Almost an hour passed, and we still had a big handful of tickets left.

Neither of us wanted to play in the bounce house. The thought of more food made me want to throw up. Even the smell of cotton candy was sickening.

The vintage lights flickered above our heads, and I was sure that must mean the festival was coming to a close.

"Last call," I said.

"There's no drinking on Main Street," Dave said. "Why do you say last call—are your legs tired?"

"No—the lights." I pointed. "You didn't see them blink?"

A strange feeling pricked the hairs on my neck when I remembered what had happened before the attempted robbery at the grocery store.

"Dave," I said, "did you ever catch that guy with the M&Ms?"

"No. I never got a good look at his face. Why, you think we should be worried about the candy here?"

I couldn't help but laugh. "No." I shook my head. "Just a feeling."

"What kind of feeling?"

My answer was interrupted by a scream down the street.

We both turned to see what the matter was but couldn't get a good look. A throng of people began hurrying in our direction. Some were barely jogging, unsure what was wrong, others were full on sprinting.

Their faces worried me most. The sprinters were scared out of their minds, looking like the doomed survivors in a zombie apocalypse movie.

"What's going on?" I tried to ask one of them.

I wanted to run with them. But Dave's instincts drove him against the wave of people. I went after him. And finally, I caught a glimpse of what had to be the problem.

Only my mind couldn't quite make sense of what was happening.

It was Trish. In the air about ten feet off the ground. She was on a broom—the old broom from the back of her store.

But why? Is she trying to out us to the world just like Summer wanted?

I was angry. Not only was she causing a stampede, she told me she'd never flown before. This seemed like a bad time to start.

With her hand over her brow, eyes scouring the crowd, she found me, then zoomed toward us. This wasn't her first time on a broom, of that I was sure. She landed like a jet on an aircraft carrier, too fast. With no arresting cable, I had to stop her with my body. We collided and fell together to the ground.

"What are you doing?"

"I came to find you," she said. "Don't worry, your Gran's okay... I think."

"What are you talking about?"

"Something's happening," she said. "Something bad."

I wanted to scream at her. But then I saw it. The clouds parted in the sky and the moon wasn't the moon it was supposed to be.

It was big and pale and round. Completely round.

That was all wrong. It had been a full moon last week when I'd waited for Dave's call.

Ahead of us, he turned. The expression on his face went from concern to shock. And his eyes were wrong, a deep yellow. Then his nose grew before our eyes.

Movies couldn't prepare me for this. He turned into a monster. Shoulders grew and his arms swung down to the road. There was so much hair. And teeth. Lots of teeth.

I would've screamed if there wasn't so much going on already.

"That's what I'm talking about," Trish yelled. "Something's wrong. It's not supposed to be a full moon for weeks. We just had one."

Dave howled, then tore away from us.

"Is he okay?" I asked.

"I think so. It's everyone else I'm worried about."

The chaos was spreading. Dave wasn't the only werewolf. There were other shifters too—foxes and goats and skunks, and some I'd never seen or heard of.

Those shifters weren't who we had to worry about. It was the people. The screaming, stampeding people.

"What should we do?" I asked Trish. "Where's Gran?"

"Your raccoon said she and Stevie went to the graveyard to sort out the moon. He told me to find you."

"What's he doing?"

She shrugged. "He's with Twinkie. They're probably doing more than we are right now."

"If only there was something we could do to make it all..."

"To make it all what?"

"To make it... Stop it! All of you!"

There was a *womp* like a shockwave through the air. The magic left my body suddenly and with force, leaving Trish and me standing in the middle of a crowd of petrified people.

"That's one way to do it," Trish said, astonished. We went around them, some in the middle of running, some yelling, some doing both. A group of teenagers huddled inside one of the booths. A family had just made it to their car before the spell took hold. Others had tried to climb up the ruins of the courthouse. Motionless. Not even gravity worked against the charm.

We found our first shifter midstride, running the opposite direction of the humans. I touched him and said, "You can move now."

His eyes darted back and forth, then his arms twitched. He shook himself out.

"Get out of here." Trish pointed.

We did the same to every shifter and werewolf we came to until finally we caught up to Dave.

"Dave, you can move," I said.

He shook his head, backing away from us.

"It's okay. I'm not afraid of you."

Maybe I should be.

"Can you talk?" Trish asked him.

He shook his head.

"Then you should get out of here," she said.

He shook his head again, pointing his paw in the direction of the bookshop.

"Okay," Trish agreed, "you hide out in there. We'll figure out the rest."

"What the heck are we going to do?" I asked her.

"A memory charm," she said confidently. "I've got one. Good job with the whole pausing time thing. I've never seen anyone do that."

"Yeah," I sighed. "I wish I could say the same."

Trish worked on her memory charm while I did something akin to Gran's cleaning for the people, returning them to normal positions as if they'd been having fun at the festival, not getting terrorized.

When Trish thought she had the memory charm worked out, I unfroze them.

It seemed to do the trick. We both sighed with relief.

We waited in the bookshop for the streets to clear. I was anxious to get back to Gran and see if she knew what had caused this whole ruckus to begin with.

Dave, still in wolf form, prowled the aisles of the shop. As a wolf, he wasn't used to being in a cooped-up space. I imagined he had as many questions as me and Trish, he just wasn't able to voice them.

We left as soon as the streets cleared, heading in the direction of Gran's house and the graveyard. There wasn't time for cars, nor did I think Dave could fit inside one. He ran. Trish had me hop on the end of her broom.

We were making good time when it happened.

I thought I saw a glint of metal in the distance, something that set my fingers to burning and my neck to prickling.

I shoved past Trish and swerved toward it. Not knowing how to drive a broom, I found the ground came up a lot faster than I thought it would. We hit a tree with an unsatisfying *thwack*.

We fell. Branches whipped at my face as I tumbled, landing knees first into the brush beneath.

"You idiot," Trish said. "You broke the broom."

"Dave," I called.

He came around the tree beside us, panting. He stopped and scouted the tree line behind me. Then he tipped his nose in the air, sniffing.

Something still felt off.

I caught the glint again in my peripheral vision. When I swung my head around to see what it was, it was too late.

Green hoodie kid. On the other side of the tree brandishing the very same gun he'd pointed at my face. Now he had it trained on Dave.

"No!" I screamed in anguish.

I leaped to push Dave away. After all, he had much more to live for than I did.

The gunshot echoed through the woods.

29

SILVER BULLET

The next few moments were a blur. The gunman disappeared into the forest while Trish and I worked to stop the bleeding on Dave—wolf Dave's shoulder.

I even took off my shirt, fixing it tightly around his hairy werewolf arm and compressing the wound. But neither of us were field medics.

What I'd give to have Jade here right now.

"We've got to get him to a hospital," I said.

Trish was the voice of reason. "Like this?"

Dave yelped in pain.

"Do you have any better ideas?"

"We need your Gran," she replied. "Do you think it's a silver bullet?"

"I don't know." I was afraid to dig it out with my finger to see. "I don't think it matters. He isn't healing himself. Do they do that?"

Trish shrugged.

"Let me think of a spell." Trish had also noticed the circle of blood on what used to be my shirt had expanded from the size of a dollar to the size of a frisbee. "If only you hadn't crashed my broom."

"If I didn't," I said, "I think he'd be in a worse state."

I didn't know if that was true. But I had to start trusting my inner witch. Every time I hadn't proved how wrong I'd been to fight my instincts.

Even with Trish there, I felt alone and helpless.

A rustling from some bushes nearby told me that wasn't true.

I turned to face it, thinking it was the kid with his gun back to finish us.

Then Brad boomed, "Your Gran is on her way. And don't worry, the moon will dissipate shortly. He'll be back to his human form—only then can you take him to the hospital."

"If Gran's coming," I said, "can't we just magic this bullet out of him?"

I figured that was why Trish needed her—for a spell or something.

"The short answer is no." Brad made his way around me, and he put a reassuring raccoon paw on my back. At once, I felt comforted, like a hug from someone you'd missed for years and years.

"He's right. We've used a lot of magic already tonight," Trish chimed in. "The good thing is, it's midsummer. Or it was. The bad thing is, we're already outside the witching hour."

Now that Trish mentioned it, I felt drained. Between freezing hundreds of people at the festival, her wiping their memories away, and whatever Gran had done, we'd used a lot of magic in a short time.

Through the trees above us, the light faded; the moon was a slice of its larger self.

Slowly, Dave's hairy face and chest began to thin. His

body contorted, and he howled with agony as he became himself again. But by the time his face was actually his face, he was unconscious. His transformation to man hadn't done anything for the wound on his shoulder. If anything, it looked worse. I rewrapped the shirt.

We didn't have to wait long after that. Soon, we heard what could only be an octogenarian hoofing it through the woods and cursing with every other step.

"I'm here. I'm here." Gran stopped to catch her breath. "Why don't you have a shirt on, dear?"

I turned her so she got a better look at Dave.

She pointed at the wound, her ruby red ring glittering in the moonlight. "Have you girls checked whether it was silver?"

We shook our heads, but Gran was already muttering a spell. "The idiot," she said. "Sterling silver. But I think we can save his life."

"How?" Trish asked.

"By calling an ambulance," Gran snapped. "Which one of you has your phone?"

Trish handed Gran her phone.

"Not me. You call it in."

Trish made the call.

"He'll be all right," Gran reassured me. "Help me get him to the road. Repeat after me."

"Light as a feather. Stiff as a board.
Let's get this oaf to a hospital ward."

"Gran!"

"It worked, didn't it?"

Dave's body floated into the air about waist high. I

pushed him by his bare feet. We found the road, and somehow, the medics were already there.

Willow's cruiser was parked behind the ambulance.

They loaded Dave up quickly. Neither medic had much to say. I wasn't sure if that was part of a spell or if perhaps they were paranormals.

Willow offered us a ride to the hospital. "Nice bra," she said, handing me a crumpled brown uniform shirt.

"And where've you been tonight, Miss Clairvoyant?" Gran asked her.

"Shrouded in mist," Willow replied. "And you?"

"Realigning the moon and the tides," Gran said matter-of-factly.

"Can you get me up to speed?" Willow asked us. "Someone's been bad. I think Dave was right. There's a hunter here."

"And they went hunting werewolf tonight," I said.

Trish and I took turns filling her in on the events of the Midsummer Festival on the way to the hospital, then told her about the kid who'd shot Dave. She was shaken. She and Dave had chosen not to go after him.

"But how is that kid so powerful?" Trish asked.

Gran didn't reply.

Lights flashing, siren on, it didn't take long to get to the hospital. Dave was already in surgery when we arrived.

"So we all agree that something crazy's going on, right?" Willow whispered. We weren't the only ones in the waiting room. I didn't think we needed to worry. The other people had their own problems—they weren't paying any attention to us.

"Right," Trish and I said in unison.

"Maybe," Gran said, out of sync.

"And you're sure it was that same kid who shot Dave?"

"Yes."

Willow nodded. Then, without warning, she froze. Her eyes went cloudy white. A second later, she sprinted for the door.

"Where are you going?" we asked.

"I've got a job to do."

"You don't want to wait and see if he's all right?"

"I already saw," she called back. "And I think I know where to find the kid."

"I'm getting a ride home," Trish said, getting up.

"Me too." Gran yawned.

"You're leaving me?"

"Willow said he's going to be all right. Our being here doesn't do him any good."

"That's not exactly what she said."

I was going to stay as long as it took—even if he was going to be all right. I needed to know Dave was going to be okay.

An hour later, groggy and yawning, Dave's sister, Imogene, arrived with his girls, all in pajamas.

Though we didn't know each other, Imogene squeezed me into the tightest of hugs.

"Is Daddy going to be okay?" Elsie asked.

I nodded, hoping it was true.

In the waiting room, the girls got comfortable—comfortable enough to sleep. Kacie snored, laying across my lap with her head in the crook of my arm.

"I appreciate you staying," Imogene kept telling me. Eventually, she nodded off too.

My eyes were tired. But my mind was too busy to sleep.

It was all tied together. Mr. Caulfield's death, whatever happened to Nell Baker in her cabin, the missing ghosts from Cyrus's vineyard, and now this.

Even the robbery—that same kid shot Dave. It couldn't be coincidence. But was he really the one behind it?

A doctor came in and said, "Marsters?"

I rubbed Imogene's shoulder, startling her awake.

We joined the doctor. "How is he?" Imogene asked.

"He lost a lot of blood, but I think he's going to pull through," the doctor said.

Imogene nodded.

"And the bullet?"

The doctor gave her a sharp look. He knew why Imogene was asking. "Nothing to worry about there. It's out of his system. We have him on a special drip to counter the effects."

"Good. Good." A tear rolled down Imogene's cheek. My eyes burned with tears of my own.

"Is there anything we can do?" Imogene asked. "Can we see him?"

"You can see him in the morning," the doctor said. "Until then, we ask relatives and friends for blood donations."

I nodded. I'd be happy to give blood. Then I gasped.

That was what we missed. Mr. Caulfield wasn't killed over a lover's quarrel with Cyrus. He was killed because of the blood he'd taken from one of Nell's animals.

And I thought I knew how to prove it.

30

USE THE FORCE, CONSTANCE

The first thing I did was call Trish—who wasn't pleased to hear my voice, it still being dark outside. But this couldn't wait. I tried to get through to Willow too. She was searching for someone far more dangerous than she probably realized. Not only some sort of wizard but a cold-blooded serial murderer to boot. One with inside knowledge of the whole town.

I sent Brad to fetch Gran and Stevie, asking that we convene in the graveyard in hopes of gleaning the information we needed.

A simple summoning spell, to prove Cyrus's innocence and learn without a doubt who this hunter was. Between the three of us we were sure to have enough magic for a summoning spell. The problem had always been knowing precisely what we were summoning. Well, I'd worked that out.

I'd worked everything out except finding a late-night ride to the graveyard. None of the ride sharing apps worked in Creel Creek, not even the shady ones.

I gave Imogene another hug, then searched the hospital closets for a broom.

If Trish could fly, so can I.

The thought turned out to be enough of a spell. After several false starts, I was flying into the gray light of morning through the swirling fog in what I hoped was the direction of the graveyard.

I landed with no fanfare just outside the gate. The broken gate, off its hinges. It lay in the dirt, barring no one's entrance.

"Brad?" I called. I'd beaten both Trish and Gran here. I was going to wait for them but impatience got the better of me.

I strode inside with purpose, making my way up the hill to the tree they'd used to transfer their gifts to me. I'd squandered them, the foresight and all of the protection.

But I could do this—I could do it on my own.

"Turned by a witch into something wrong.
Used by a vampire all along.
He was the one who chose to stay.
Who was the one who got away?"

The wind whipped over the hill, stirring the branches of the tree. It ruffled my hair and whispered in my ear...

Haaaalllll.

That wasn't right. I wanted to ask the spirits again. I wanted to tell them they were wrong. My magic failed.

A shiver ran down my spine. Striding up the hill wearing a cloak and holding a shoulder-height black staff, complete with a skull on the tip, was Hal Aaron. Halitosis Hal himself.

"You?" I accused.

"Me." A wicked smile revealed those gross mossy teeth.

"I, uh, I—" I struggled to find words. "I'm warning you," I said.

Isn't that what you're supposed to do when you feel threatened—threaten back?

He paid the threat no mind.

"I'm not alone," I warned him. I was completely alone. "Trish will be here soon. Gran will—"

"Oh, Trish, I need you at the graveyard right now." Hal mimicked my voice to a T.

"It's too early for this, Constance. Fine. I'll be there." This time, he used Trish's voice. The voice on the other end of the line—back when I was sure that it was the kid in the green hoodie who'd done everything. Back when I was sure Trish was on her way.

"How?"

"A spell," he said. "I cast it when I put my number into your phone."

I put a hand to my mouth.

"Do you remember asking what I said? I thought for sure you'd figured me out."

At the time, it had seemed inconsequential. Getting him out of my hair. I had no intention of calling Hal. He'd tricked me—and probably spied on me as well.

Reality set in like a bucket of ice water dumped over my head. If it was Hal on the phone when I'd called Trish, then it was probably Hal on the phone when I called Willow as well.

"Now you're catching on," he sneered.

It's okay, I thought. *I still have Gran*. Brad was going to get her. He couldn't stop that. *Could he?*

"Oh, you don't get it, do you?" He fake pouted. "I know

all your moves. I banished your familiar to a realm he'll never find his way out of."

I was too scared to scream.

"Lucky for your Gran, the protection on her house is solid. Unlucky for you, she's fast asleep. Now, to matters at hand."

"What—what do you want? What's this all about?"

He'd already gotten away with the murder of Mr. Caulfield. There was nothing I could offer him, but nothing I thought I'd done to deserve a gruesome end. I wondered if this was still about a date.

"Your power." Hal dug his staff into the ground. "Did you know you can take a witch's power in her first year? It's a very special year, turning forty. I'll have it from you now."

Hal leveled his staff at my chest. But he came to a stop a few feet away, almost like an invisible barrier was blocking him. He backed up, then tried to round the invisible barrier. This time, he was flattened.

Trish's protection spell.

He tried again and again. The spell was going to hold no matter what Hal did.

"How'd you do it?" I tried to get him talking, to buy time to think.

"Do what?" He jabbed at the air with his staff.

"How'd you do all of this?"

"I found the book," he said. "The witch's book. You know, she didn't even miss me when I escaped. I think she let it happen. She knew what I was capable of."

"And how did you find the book?"

"It fell on my doorstep, you could say. I used it to make the potion. I'd heard the witch threaten to use it one day—one day when her side of the bargain wasn't such a good deal."

"But why? Why kill Mr. Caulfield?"

"Why not?" Hal asked. He struggled, trying to force himself through the spell. "Caulfield was an insect. That tick didn't even know I existed. He didn't know he'd nourished himself for years on my blood. He treated me like a lowlife when it was him that was lower than low."

"Why didn't you stop there?"

"Stop? I couldn't stop. I had the book. I used it to spell your phone. I used it to guide the mind of that idiot kid who lives down my street. He was always trespassing, always looking for trouble. So I gave him some. He's useless now. This isn't."

Hal threw down the staff and pulled out the gun.

"It worked on a werewolf," he spat. "I'm sure it'll do okay on a witch."

I didn't have time to think. I didn't have time to do anything but react. To remove the threat—cereal eating, not so innocent, power hungry Hal.

It wasn't much of an idea. I just had to do what had already been done to him, probably a thousand times. Just like Nell Baker.

Sure, it was probably a temporary solution. It's possible he knew how to counter the spell. But when a man is pointing a gun at you, every second is precious.

I wished I knew how to go invisible again.

I only had one chance.

One shot.

An owl hooted in the distance, reminding me that I wasn't alone. Maybe someone was watching over me somehow.

My mom.

"A rat with wings, a rodent that sings," I chanted without thinking.

"He deserves this fate,
for breaking the gate.
For being a brat,
Halitosis Hal is a bat."

The transformation happened rapidly. In bat form, he beat his wings wildly, flew high, and attempted to dive bomb my head. Trish's spell held.

"Hoo, hoo."

The owl swooped in, all talons and wings in the morning light. It snatched bat-Hal out of the air and was off, disappearing into the wood.

31

THE WRONG DOUG

"Pause. Now, rewind. Play."

"Dave, I've already told you the whole thing twice."

"But Willow hasn't heard it." Dave motioned at the deputy hovering by the doorway.

"She was the first one I told."

"It's true." Willow agreed.

"Listen," Dave said, "I'm on a lot of pain medication. I can hardly tell you apart from the other you." He gestured with the finger wearing an oxygen monitor. "There's dueling Willows. And there's three of Trish. Can't you just humor me?"

"Come on, Constance." Trish nudged me. "It's not going to hurt anything."

"Except my voice." I rubbed my neck. Then I explained it one more time from the moment Dave transformed into a wolf to the moment I turned Hal into a bat—a bat probably eaten by an owl.

"And you like owls?"

"My mother liked owls."

Medicated and groggy, Dave didn't remember much of what happened. Trish and I met Willow at his hospital bedside. Gran and Stevie stayed at the bookstore, searching the texts she had on hand. They'd resolved to find and retrieve Brad from whatever plane of existence Hal had sent him to. It would be easier if we had the book. But even with a thorough search of his squalid house and several summoning spells, neither Trish nor I could find it.

"So, you're saying it was Hal the whole time?" Dave asked again.

"I think so."

"And he was Nell's first," Trish added. "The timeline makes sense. You remember when his mother died?"

"I remember," Dave said. "And I remember thinking it was all sorts of fishy. But I wasn't the sheriff then. I didn't have a lot of pull."

"Wouldn't Nell know he went missing?" Willow asked.

"She did," I told them. "He said as much. He said she knew what he was capable of, but she didn't care.

"So, he wrote that story and sent it to Jade."

"Nell always did have a screw loose," Trish said. "I never knew how loose."

"I never met the woman," Dave said.

"That's probably not true," Trish replied. "Nell had this spell that made everyone forget about her a few minutes after talking to her. It got on my nerves, so I found a counterspell."

"Well, it's a little late to worry about her," Dave said. "And probably too late for Hal. Not much I can do without him here to answer a few questions."

"We could exhume his mother's body," Willow said. "Run his mother's DNA against the blood stored in the freezer."

"Good idea, deputy. Speaking of exhumation reminds me we need to release a certain someone."

Willow nodded. "Just say the word, and I'll put the paperwork through."

"The word," Dave said.

She rolled her eyes.

"What about the boy?" Dave asked. "The one who shot me."

"I found him last night—right where my vision said I would," Willow said. "He's in a room down the hall, cuffed to the bed. Just in case."

"Good thinking," Dave said. "If y'all don't mind, I need a minute with Constance?"

I had the heart-sinking feeling of getting pulled over again. His injuries were at least partially my fault. Hal was after me, not him. He was after my power.

"None of this is your fault," Dave said. "None of it."

"But I—"

"No buts. I did this to myself. If I hadn't tried the daylight potion, I wouldn't have changed like I did."

"You what?"

He shook me off. "It was an experiment. A dumb one. On a regular night, I would have been able to talk to you. But that false full moon combined with the potion's side effects, well, it wasn't my brightest idea ever."

"You dumb, dumb werewolf," I scolded him.

"Can this dumb werewolf get another date? Maybe this one won't end in mayhem."

"You promised me there wouldn't be any mayhem last time."

"Okay. No promises then." He smiled.

I left him to get some rest.

With Hal out of the picture, there was no need to push

his recovery. He needed to heal before I let him help me with my quest to find out more about the Faction—if I let him help. I'd already put his family through so much. I wasn't eager to do it again.

I was going to find out what happened to my mom, no matter what. I couldn't shake the feeling that she'd been watching over me in my fight against Hal.

On my way out, I passed green hoodie's room. The chart on his door said his name was Doug.

Poor Doug.

He was just a pawn.

We spent the evening at Bewitched Books, drinking Cyrus's red wine and going through old spell books. We didn't find anything that might bring back my lost familiar.

I actually missed having a trash panda steal my covers. We finished the night with a new episode of *Creel Creek After Dark*. I hoped there was nothing new from the wonder twins, Athena and Ivana—or at least nothing about the Midsummer Festival. Trish was talking about wiping memories around town just in case.

When my eyes finally closed, I dropped into a dream-packed sleep. The images churned like the ocean in a storm. Hal turning into a bat then changing back. *Why did I pick a bat?* I'd wondered about it all day. Did I know that owls ate bats? Surely not.

I eventually realized why—he killed a vampire, so it seemed apropos.

I dreamed about a raccoon, then the shadow of a man, or not a man, a shadow with feathered wings.

I woke up hearing my father's voice, a distant sound.

32

CREEL CREEK AFTER DARK EPISODE 47

IT'S GETTING LATE.

Very late.
The creeping dread of tomorrow haunts your dreams.
It's dark out. Are you afraid?
Welcome to Creel Creek After Dark.

Athena: I'm your host Athena Hunter. With me, as always, is the lovely Ivana Steak.

Ivana: That's right, I'm Ivana Steak. And can I just say, it's been a weird few weeks?

Athena: In a place like Creel Creek, that's saying something.

Ivana: I know, right.

Athena: Today's episode is a follow-up to episode forty-four. That's right. This week, we received another anonymous story.

Ivana: A true story.

Athena: Is it really?

Ivana: You know what I think?

Athena: No, what?

Ivana: I believe we have to find our own truth. That's

exactly what this podcast is about. Finding the truth here in Creel Creek.

Athena: Without further ado, here is *Exit the Hunter* by author unknown.

THE HUNTER LEFT Creel Creek feeling satisfied. They'd be back. And with them, they'd bring more pain to the *unconventional* residents of the town.

With the vampire gone and the wolf incapacitated, the witches were next on the list. The witches were always the last to go.

From afar, the Hunter had watched the new witch come into her powers. She'd known nothing, at first. No magic. No history.

And how fair a fight would that be? the Hunter wondered.

The new witch had proven herself quickly. Time and again, she'd proven more than capable. She'd learned to use her magic to protect herself, to protect the town. And she'd taken on a warlock.

Soon enough, the fight would be even. And that's when the Hunter would return.

THE END

If you enjoyed this book, why not leave a review? They're vital for other readers to learn about my work.

MORE CREEL CREEK

Explore Creel Creek through the eyes of its residents with exclusive episodes of *Creel Creek After Dark* when you sign up for the newsletter.

NEVER BEEN HEXED

WITCHING HOUR
BOOK TWO

COVER
COMING
SOON

GHOST DAD

Even in the midst of a crisis, sleep is a necessity.

And sleep called to me. It begged. Reluctantly, I heeded its call. After going several nights without, staying up all hours reading from spell books and researching potions, I was no closer to an answer than I had been when I started.

Unlike eating—or other forms of self-care—a body can force sleep. No matter the amount of caffeine in my bloodstream, no matter the determination I had to struggle through one more page, my eyes scanning over the same words over and over, my body was ready.

I turned off my lamp and crashed into bed, allowing sleep to wash over me like a wave. The gears in my mind finally slowed to a stop. With one deep breath, I was out.

"Constance." My father's voice mingled with the dream I was having.

Maybe it wasn't a dream but a memory. My mother's glassy blue eyes peered down at a younger, smaller version of myself. Current me, at nearly six-foot tall, wouldn't need to crane my neck to see into those eyes. They were so pale. I could almost see into her. My mother's eyes really were windows into her soul—a soul that went missing shortly before I'd turned ten years old, over thirty years ago now.

"Constance," my father said again, distant—like maybe he was in the next room. Like he was calling to me in the memory itself. I fought the urge to leave my mother's side. I wanted to stay. I wanted to be with her, if only for a little while longer. My father could wait.

"I need you to wake up."

Isn't that how all dreams end—with a need to wake up. It's never a want.

My eyes flitted open. They struggled, going wide and squinting against the pale luminescence in the room. It was still dark outside, but the room was oddly bright.

My body protested, having not had near the right amount of sleep. I ached all over. My back. My knees. My hips. My mind was much the same, not yet engaged with the guilt it had been feeling over the past few days—that guilt being the reason I couldn't sleep and why my bouts of insomnia were at an all-time high.

"Five more minutes," I said out loud.

"Constance." It was my dad's voice again.

Present.

Here.

I jerked up, fully awake, threw the bedsheet off me, and scrambled for my laptop, thinking I must've left it open. Usually, we FaceTimed or did Skype calls. I didn't remember him telling me he was going to call. But he must've.

I squeezed my burning eyes closed against the wisp of pale energy in the room, not yet registering what it was. Not until it said my name again. Not until I turned to face the pale figure full on. The ghost of my father.

Henry Campbell, age sixty-eight, should've been at his home outside San Diego, California. Like me, he should've been asleep in his bed. Instead, he stood at the edge of my bed, made up of what looked like water vapor—like a bright blue mist, fading into fuzzy outlines at the fringes.

He wasn't wearing any clothes. His body was just a shape of a man below the neck. No muscles, no skeletal structure. He was a blur of a man. His hands and feet were barely realized. When he moved, they were like tendrils of water vapor, of mist, slowly catching up with the rest of him.

In life, my father had grown old. His hair was all gray, almost white. He wore glasses. And often, he sported a full beard, framing his honker of a nose and thin lips. His eyes had been a brownish gray.

This face was nothing like that. It was more like the man I remembered from my youth—from around the time of that memory of my mother.

I would've screamed had the recognition not struck me into a stupor. The hairs all over my body were standing on end. Then I realized that the hairs all over my body were in plain sight. In my sleep, I'd taken off my nightshirt. The heat of July made the second story of my grandmother's house, where I slept in her spare bedroom, sweltering hot.

Frozen in the middle of the room, laptop in hand, I stood wide-eyed in just a light pink thong.

The specter face of my father winced. "You don't wear PJs anymore, sweetheart?"

I grimaced. The bed's comforter, that I'd half-kicked on the floor, dangled at the end of the bed. I wrapped it around my shoulders like a shawl. I was pretty confident this was just another dream—one of those *Inception* deals—but I had to take precautions.

"Dad?"

It's hard to know what you'd do or say when confronted by a real ghost until it happens.

"It's me, honey."

"Dad, you're a..."

"A ghost. I know."

I pinched the skin on my forearm. It didn't hurt. Then I realized I hadn't pinched hard enough. The next time, I meant it. The next time, I felt it. Pain throbbed from the spot.

Still, I wasn't convinced.

I'd read somewhere that one way to tell if you're dreaming is to find a clock. My phone would have to do. Except I couldn't remember what to do when looking at the clock. It looked normal. It looked like several hours before sunrise.

"You're not dreaming," the ghost said.

"That sounds like something someone would say in a dream."

"You're right. It does, doesn't it? Tell ya what—I'll prove it. Ask me something. Ask me anything."

"That doesn't work either," I said. "If I ask you something, you'll either know it because you know it or because—"

"Because I'm your consciousness. Yeah. I get it." He nodded, his face blurring up and down. "Maybe it doesn't matter if you think you're dreaming or not. Either way tomorrow comes—and with it the news."

"What news?"

"The news of my death."

A sting of tears rushed to bursting, streaming down my cheeks. I knew I wasn't dreaming. Those tears were real.

"You can't be."

"I am, sweetie," he said.

"But how? And how are you a ghost?"

In any normal circumstance, I'd probably be questioning this whole scenario—I'd think it was some joke. But my life had taken several twisting turns over the past few weeks. First, I'd learned that I was a witch—from a long line of witches, including my grandmother and my mother. To top that off, my long dead mother might not be so dead after all. She'd gone missing after starting a job for a mysterious paranormal organization known as the Faction.

Then, before I could even come into my powers, I stumbled across the body of my former boss, a vampire. I got dragged into his murder investigation by the local sheriff, a werewolf. A ruggedly handsome werewolf.

And those powers came in handy once I had them. I'd almost been killed for them.

So, a ghost in my bedroom hardly seemed out of the norm. Just another night in my midlife curse.

I shuddered as this new anxiety mixed with the old. My father was dead. He was a ghost.

"That's why I came here," he said. "They're going to tell you I died of natural causes. A heart attack or something like that."

"But?"

"But it's not true. I don't know how I died, Constance. I heard voices. Unnatural voices."

"Who?"

"I don't know who." His voice sounded distant, like an echo of what I was used to hearing. And it started to fade even from that. "Honey, there's something I've been meaning to talk to you about."

I nodded encouragingly. I wanted him to just spit it out. Whatever he wanted to say, we were going to figure this out. We were going to figure it all out—who killed him and how.

I was going to run to Gran and see if there was any way of changing him back, although I'd seen *Practical Magic* enough times to know that probably wasn't a good idea.

"Your mom," he continued, "she told me something once." He tried to whisper and it barely reached my ears. "She told me she was a witch."

"She was," I said. "I'm one too."

He didn't acknowledge my words. He waved his phantom arm from side to side in front of his face. "This form doesn't want to stay here. Not long."

"What do you need to tell me?" I pressed.

"I think… I think maybe I was killed by magic."

It made no sense. There was no way he could know that. And yet.

"I have to go," he said in a rush.

"No. Don't go," I pleaded even more hurriedly. "We can fix this. You just have to stay here. I'll get Gran."

If anyone would know how to fix this, it'd be my eighty-something-year-old grandmother.

"I'll try to come back," Dad said.

"You will? Promise me."

"I'll find a way."

The bright glow that had once filled his form dipped inward, dimming to a glowing ball at the center of his chest. Then the ghostly form of my father winked out of existence. Possibly, for good.

Constance and the gang are back in
Never Been Hexed: Witching Hour Book 2, Available Soon.

ALSO BY CHRISTINE ZANE THOMAS

Witching Hour starring 40 year old witch Constance Campbell

Book 1: Midlife Curses

Book 2: Never Been Hexed

Book 3: Must Love Charms

Book 4: You've Got Spells

Tessa Randolph Cozy Mysteries written with Paula Lester

Grim and Bear It

The Scythe's Secrets

Reap What She Sows

Foodie File Mysteries starring Allie Treadwell

The Salty Taste of Murder

A Choice Cocktail of Death

A Juicy Morsel of Jealousy

The Bitter Bite of Betrayal

Comics and Coffee Case Files starring Kirby Jackson and Gambit

Book 1: Marvels, Mochas, and Murder

Book 2: Lattes and Lies

Book 3: Cold Brew Catastrophe

Book 4: Decaf Deceit

ABOUT CHRISTINE ZANE THOMAS

Christine Zane Thomas is the pen name of a husband and wife team. A shared love of mystery and sleuths spurred the creation of their own mysterious writer alter-ego.

While not writing, they can be found in northwest Florida with their two children, their dachshund Queenie, and schnauzer Tinker Bell. When not at home, their love of food takes them all around the South. Sometimes they sprinkle in a trip to Disney World. Food and Wine is their favorite season.

ACKNOWLEDGMENTS

Thanks to Ellen Campbell who edited this book. To Sara Johnson for proofreading. To Jason and Hillary for beta reads, helping to steer this book in the right direction. And as always to my family and friends who help support my writing pursuits.

Made in the USA
Monee, IL
16 June 2020